NOTE

Dear Reader,

When I finished writing *Heart of the Sun Warrior*, I found it hard to leave the characters and wanted to spend a little more time with them—imagining their lives in the future, and what might have prompted their decisions in the past. I never dreamed these stories would become a book, accompanied by such beautiful illustrations.

All my personal proceeds from *Tales of the Celestial Kingdom* will be donated to charity, and I hope in this way to be able to give something back. Thank you for your support of my stories, and for the chance to share them.

With love,

TALES

OF THE

CELESTIAL
KINGDOM

TALES
OF THE
CELESTIAL
KINGDOM

SUE LYNN TAN

HARPER Voyager

An Imprint of HarperCollins Publishers

TALES OF THE CELESTIAL KINGDOM. Copyright © 2024 by Sue Lynn Tan. All rights reserved. Printed in the United States of America. No part of this book may be used or reproduced in any manner whatsoever without written permission except in the case of brief quotations embodied in critical articles and reviews. For information, address HarperCollins Publishers, 195 Broadway, New York, NY 10007.

HarperCollins books may be purchased for educational, business, or sales promotional use. For information, please email the Special Markets Department at SPsales@harpercollins.com.

Harper Voyager and design are trademarks of HarperCollins Publishers LLC.

FIRST EDITION

Designed by Jennifer Chung
Map design by Virginia Allyn
Illustrations © Kelly Chong
Title spread art © Xinling yi fang/Shutterstock

Library of Congress Cataloging-in-Publication Data has been applied for.

ISBN 978-0-06-332669-9

24 25 26 27 28 LBC 6 5 4 3 2

To my father who taught me to look up at the skies,
and to my mother for keeping my feet on the ground.

CONTENTS

꧁

Map   *x*

Author's Note   *xiii*

—— DUSK ——

Chang'e | 嫦娥: Rise of the Sunbirds   *3*

Houyi | 后羿: The Ten Suns   *15*

Chang'e | 嫦娥: Goddess of the Moon   *29*

—— TWILIGHT ——

Liwei | 力伟: The Snow Ginseng Root   *47*

Wenzhi | 文智: Battle with the Bone Devil   *59*

Shuxiao | 淑晓: Return to the Jade Palace   *77*

Liwei | 力伟: A Rival's Spirit   *97*

—— DAWN ——

Wenzhi | 文智: Sun Moon Teahouse   *115*

Xingyin | 星银: Home   *127*

Acknowledgments   *149*

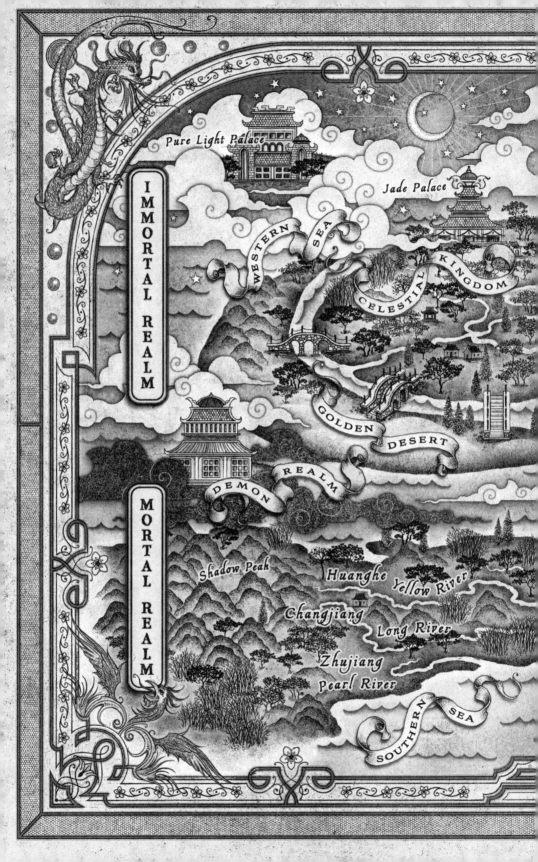

AUTHOR'S NOTE

WHEN I WROTE *DAUGHTER OF THE MOON GODDESS*, I never imagined the incredible and emotional journey the books would take me on, that this treasured compilation would exist. The first few stories in *Tales of the Celestial Kingdom* were written during a break between the duology, and there was no real plan for them. Since then, I've added to the tales, drawing upon certain moments across the books to shed a little more light upon the characters and their relationships.

As there are spoilers for the duology within, I wanted to share a little about the arrangement of this compilation. The three stories in "Dusk" are reimaginings of the original legend that inspired the books, a prequel in a way, reinterpreting the myth in the world of the Celestial Kingdom—and these can be read without prior knowledge of the duology. The first two tales in "Twilight" explore blossoming relationships in *Daughter of the Moon Goddess,* expanding upon moments as the ginseng root that was gifted to the Celestial Empress, and the monster recounted by Xingyin upon her return to the Jade Palace as the First Archer. The remaining stories, including those in "Dawn," would ideally be read after *Heart of the Sun Warrior* as they contain major spoilers.

In this compilation, we explore multiple viewpoints of different characters—Chang'e and Houyi, Liwei, Wenzhi and Shuxiao—and the epilogue is the only story told from Xingyin's point of view. It was exciting to write from other characters' perspectives, giving voice to their thoughts and delving deeper into who they are. Within their pages, there are some differences given the narrator, and reflecting who the character is at a point in time—what they know and what they've gone through. While many of the characters have changed over the course of the books, some undergo greater transformation than others.

The tale of Chang'e and Houyi is one I have always loved, a Mid-Autumn legend that I grew up with, that has stayed with me over time. Many variations of the myth exist, and I always wondered if there might be more to it—for Chang'e to take the elixir and leave her beloved husband. While I wanted to honor the existing legend in *Daughter of the Moon Goddess*, I also wanted to take it in a new direction of a heroine whose path was yet uncharted.

I always imagined Xingyin's tale as a duology, with each book centered on different elements of the mythology, and was thrilled when my editor shared the vision. Chang'e and Houyi each have their own part in the myth, starting from their life together as mortals, to when their paths diverge—one ascending to the skies, the other remaining on earth. Just as *Daughter of the Moon Goddess* was inspired by Chang'e, I wanted *Heart of the Sun Warrior* to delve deeper into the legend of Houyi. For those who have not read the sequel, elements of the plot will be revealed below as I share some of its inspiration.

The duology also weaves in other Chinese myths, namely the Four Dragons in *Daughter of the Moon Goddess*, while *Heart of the Sun Warrior* features another lesser-known figure of Mid-Autumn legend, that of the woodcutter on the moon. Some believed that after gaining immortality, Chang'e lived on the moon, accompanied by only a rabbit and the woodcutter, who had offended the Jade Emperor and was sentenced to chop an enchanted tree for eternity. The legend diverges into multiple variations, with the woodcutter's wrongdoing ranging from laziness to killing his wife's lover. For the latter, I wondered how this crime of passion might twist his heart and mind, how it might shape his future if he allowed it to consume him.

Another source of inspiration is the Terracotta Army, the thousands of clay soldiers constructed to guard the tomb of the first emperor of China. They have always fascinated me, their history and purpose, the intricacy and details of their crafting.

In these stories you will find magical kingdoms, grand battles, cunning monarchs, and noble warriors, yet what lies at the heart of this duology is love—both romantic and familial. I believe love is mysterious, complex, unexpected—far more gray than black-and-white—something that grows and evolves, as do we. And I believe the characters followed the path that was most true to who they were, who they grew into, which may not be who they started out as at the beginning.

Xingyin's story is perhaps less of a fairy tale than that of a woman fighting for what she believes in as she seeks the answers to her own life, accepting that she might never have them all, learning what makes her happy, being courageous enough to reach for it—and despite the challenges she encounters, remaining hopeful for what tomorrow may bring.

These characters have come to mean so much to me, it is hard to recall a time when they were not part of my life, and I've loved writing them with all my heart. I am thankful for everyone who made this possible, and to you for wanting to read more of the Celestial Kingdom, and I hope you will enjoy returning there once again.

TALES

OF THE

CELESTIAL

KINGDOM

DUSK

CHANG'E | 嫦娥
RISE OF THE SUNBIRDS

A prequel to *Daughter of the Moon Goddess*,
reimagining the myth of the ten sunbirds, set in the
world of the Celestial Kingdom.

———

L IGHT FILTERED THROUGH THE GAUZE screens that covered the windows, the wooden frames latticed in a pattern of squares. I blinked, trying to adjust to the dazzling brightness, my mind still sluggish. Slumber had been hard won—I'd slept with the curtains pulled back from the posts, though it did little good. While I did not perspire easily, my silk robe clung to me, damp with sweat. Breathing in, I almost choked on the air, suffused with a brittle heat unusual in the beginning of spring when the days still bore a remnant of winter. My body felt heavy, each movement languorous, as I pushed myself from the bed. I was alone, Houyi's blanket still neatly folded at the foot of the bed. Had he not returned during the night?

Walking to the windows, I pushed them apart, quickly—before the wood seared my fingers. Through the slender opening, I glimpsed a crack of sky, ablaze with vermilion flame. I dropped my gaze at once to protect my sight. How long had it been this way, the heat intensifying without relief, day blending seamlessly into night until I could no longer tell them apart? The sun never set—if it still existed—like it was a yolk punctured,

3

spilling across the heavens. It had never been like this, not even in the most scorching of summers. Tendrils of premonition curled in my stomach, spiraling unbound like coils of smoke. This strange and terrible phenomenon did not seem to be of our realm.

If only Houyi were here. He would calm my fears, he would know what to do, always so steady and decisive. Even the king sought and treasured his opinion. At times, my husband's iron assurance and certainty grated on me, particularly in the moments we disagreed—but now I wished I could lean on it, to have him close when danger hovered around us. Yet since the skies had turned to liquid fire, he was often away at the king's behest. They had sought the counsel of the wisest elders in the land, of soothsayers and fortune-tellers, yet none possessed the answers needed.

I did not know how long I waited by the window; time had lost its meaning with the position of the sun unknown. At last, familiar steps trod along the stone path outside, firm and quick. Hastily, I tucked in the loose strands of my hair and discarded my robe for a fresh one, a green silk embroidered with lotuses.

The wooden door swung open, my pulse leaping as it always did at the sight of my husband, even when streaked with sweat and dust. His black hair was coiled into a topknot, held in place with a band of silver, and he stood as straight as an arrow. His fine gray robe was wrinkled and scuffed at the hem, fastened with a leather belt studded with jade. Many considered his face to be strong rather than pleasing, with those sharp cheekbones, that distinct cleft in his broad chin. Beneath winged eyebrows, his dark eyes gleamed—his penetrating gaze that struck such terror into an enemy's heart, even as it quickened mine.

He unstrapped his sword, sheathed in a scabbard of gold and ebony, then set it on the table by the doorway—along with a silver bow he unslung from his shoulder, intricately carved, the ends curving to sharp points. I had never seen it before, perhaps it was a gift from the king. Later, I would take his weapons and polish them. A servant might have done it, but there was satisfaction in caring for my husband's possessions. Particularly those that kept him safe, that brought him home to me each day.

As he came toward me, I wanted to press closer to him, to drink in his scent, laced with the spice that was his alone. Already the air seemed less stifling, my mood lighter, my fears less dire.

"Chang'e, sit. The doctor said you must rest, for both you and our child," he told me gently.

"I am well," I said. "Lying abed all day would be more of a strain." My stomach was still barely curved. It was early yet, though he treated me like I was made of porcelain. I was fortunate to be spared the nausea that plagued others, just an occasional fatigue that tugged at my limbs.

He smiled at me, but his gaze remained troubled.

"What's the matter, Houyi? Why did you not return last night?" Not an accusation but an invitation to speak his cares. He preferred to spare me their burden when all I wanted was to share them.

"I have discovered the source of the calamity that plagues our realm," he said gravely.

"Have we angered the gods?" What else could these raging skies of flame mean?

His face darkened. "It is the sunbirds."

"Sunbirds?" I frowned, trying to recall the stories I had heard of them.

"Yes. All ten have risen at once."

"Ten?" I gasped. "I thought they were just a myth."

He shook his head. "They are real. Down here, you can only see their fire, but higher in the mountains is where you can make out their forms."

One sun sufficed to light the world, already causing famine and drought during the worst seasons. How might we escape the destruction of *ten*?

"Can't we tell the sunbirds to stop? Maybe they do not realize the harm they are causing."

"I tried. Either they did not hear me, or they did not care." He glanced out of the window, his expression grim. "Yet how can they not know? The devastation is impossible to ignore."

Despair gripped me. "We can't survive this heat for much longer," I whispered.

He reached out and laid his palm over mine. Even after these years together, his touch still thrilled and comforted me. I turned my hand over and threaded my fingers through his—roughly callused, yet more slender than one might have expected of his warrior's form.

"I will face the sunbirds. I will stop them." He spoke with unflinching resolve as though it were a trivial matter.

"No." My refusal came swiftly, so harshly spoken it startled me as much as him. I was no novice to danger, its constant shadow looming over our marriage. A demanding mistress, prying my husband from my arms in the form of terrifying beasts, great wars, and violent uprisings. Each time, I had embraced him and sent him off with a warm smile to bolster his spirits, swallowing my tears until he had left.

Not now. This danger was greater than anything he had ever faced. The sunbirds were said to be divine creatures, the children of an ancient goddess who dwelled in the heavens. Even if my husband could defeat such powerful beings—victory would come at a steep price, for whose wrath might he incur?

Terror flooded me, relentless and cold. "Why you? Why not another?" A selfish sentiment but an honest one. I asked it even as I knew his mind was made up. No matter the danger, Houyi would never shirk his duty. Moreover, who else could face the monsters that plagued our skies? He was a hero of the people, a legend of our realm . . . but for today, I just wanted him to be my husband.

"I must do this." He spoke gently but firmly.

His gaze rested on the tea set before us, of porcelain rimmed with gold. Our cupboards bulged with sacks of rice, beans, dried fish, cured meats—provisions against times of misfortune. A servant had laid a meal on the rosewood table: a whole chicken braised with herbs, a plate of jade-green stalks, and silken bean curd so soft, it seemed to quiver beneath our breath.

The foremost commander of the king's army wanted for nothing.

"We are lucky. For now," he said in a low voice. "But the rivers have run dry, the fields are barren. Famine is already upon us, and it will reach here soon. As I rode across villages, the cries of the people rang in my ears, the sunken cheeks of their children tore at my soul. The poor are the first to suffer, but death hovers over us all."

I longed to cry out: *What about your wife and unborn child? What if something happened to* you? But I let the words fade upon my tongue even as tears pricked my eyes. I was used to locking my fears within, rather than burdening another.

He plucked a crimson peony from the vase—the last unwilted bloom from our garden—snapped off part of its stalk, and slid it into my hair, as he had often done during the early days of our courtship. Sometimes, when he was away, I would tuck a flower there to remind myself of him. But there were no flowers here anymore, just their withered stalks.

"Chang'e, I will be safe. I will return. I promise I will never leave you and our child alone in this world."

I tried again. "But the sunbirds are beloved by the gods."

His lips lifted into a small smile. "Maybe the gods favor me, too."

A gold chain gleamed at his neck, one I had not seen before. Was it a good-luck charm? Something he had bought from the market to ward off evil? I would drape him in them, if only they would bring him back to me, unharmed.

He continued, "I do not intend to attack the sunbirds; I still hope to reason with them."

What if they will not listen? But I said no more; it would do no good when he was resolved. I would not spoil our time together, fighting a battle I could not win. Nor would I be his weakness, weighing him down when he needed to be strong in body, mind, and heart. And so, I smiled and nodded, serving him the choicest parts of our meal, keeping my tears within me as we went to bed. And if I held him a little tighter that night, he did not remark upon it.

The next morning, I rose early, my skin already slicked with sweat. Houyi had covered our windows with thick cloth, stuffed into the crevices of our door to block out the relentless heat, clinging to any shadow of coolness. Even at night, there was no respite from the sunbirds' torment. A heaviness sank over me, the knowledge that my husband was right. I could not be selfish; I could not be a coward. He was the only one who could offer us a sliver of hope. If left unchecked, the sunbirds would destroy us all.

A servant appeared at the doorway, roused by my footsteps, her eyes still lidded with slumber. I waved her away, back to bed. With my own hands, I prepared a pot of congee cooked with the remains of the chicken from our evening meal, flavored with wolfberries and slices of ginger. I rolled dough into thin sticks, frying them to a crisp golden brown—but not too long so their insides remained soft and chewy. These I served with a bowl of eggs, stewed in aromatic tea and herbs until the whites were stained brown.

My husband ate silently, his brow furrowed in thought, his mind already plotting ahead. For a moment, pity sparked in me for the foes he faced. His reputation as the greatest warrior in the realm was well earned. He would vanquish the sunbirds; he would return. Such assurances I repeated to myself over and over as I walked him to the doorway, gripping his helmet between my hands until the metal formed dents in my skin. As he lowered his head, I slid it over his soft hair, which I had run my fingers through just the night before. He leaned toward me then, pressing his lips against mine, hard and urgent as though savoring the taste of me. My restraint shattered as I threw my arms around his neck to clutch him tighter. He clasped me to him, his armor grinding against my flesh, but I did not flinch, reveling in the intimacy.

Those who thought me aloof had never seen me with my husband.

"Wait for me here," he murmured into my ear. "Don't see me out; the heat is too fierce."

His hand slid up to my cheek, then down again to the curve of my stomach. He inclined his head once, then strode through the doorway into the blinding light beyond. Beneath the shelter of our roof, I stared after him as he mounted his horse and grasped the reins. The horse swung around obediently, galloping away as it kicked up pebbles and clumps of browned grass from our once verdant courtyard. As the sun blazed down upon my husband, something glittered from his back—the silver bow I had glimpsed yesterday. How I prayed its aim would be true.

He will return, I reminded my treacherous and doubting mind a hundred times over the course of the day. He had never broken a promise to me. Intermittently, I cursed the selfish sunbirds for the suffering they had caused us. Why had they risen all at once? Why did they not cease their wickedness? Why did the Emperor of Heaven not strike them down with his might?

At once, I rebuked myself for such dangerous thoughts, a frantic unease writhing in my stomach. I hurried to the altar, my fingers fumbling for the incense sticks, lighting three as I fell to my knees, inhaling their fragrant smoke. My lips moved in a quick prayer as I bent myself over, touching my forehead to the ground. Since discovering I was with child, I had made offerings to the gods daily—praying for our health, a safe birth, a strong child. With so much at stake, I dared not anger the gods, even as my husband rode out to challenge their own.

Rising, I made my way listlessly to a chair—for the first time feeling that the weight of our child was more a burden than a blessing. I sipped my tea as I fanned myself. It did little good against the heat, but the rhythmic movements yielded some comfort. Spread across the wooden blades was a beautiful painting of plum blossoms, their vibrant petals dusted with pale snow, caught among the dark branches. A gift from my husband that I cherished more than pearls or jade because of the words he had spoken then.

"Why plum blossoms?" I had asked curiously. It had been spring, the season of peonies and magnolias.

"Because they remind me of you," he had replied. "Thriving even when buried in ice, their frail petals concealing a core of strength."

It was one of the things I loved about him; that he did not speak of my beauty alone as my other suitors had done, writing absurd poems to the arch of my brow, the curve of my lips. It was why I had waited for him those years he was away, knowing in my heart that I would marry no other.

My mind drifted back to the danger that awaited my husband. Squinting, I peeked through the window at the fiery sky. How might a mortal bring down a creature of heaven? While my husband was no ordinary mortal—rather, the greatest archer in the world—talent was not the only decider of fate. Luck, too often, dealt the deciding blow.

Hours passed. Half a day, perhaps? The afternoon meal was left untouched on the table, the once soft dumplings turned stiff and dry. I dared not venture into the scorching heat of the courtyard. Once, it had bloomed with flowers; once, the sunken hole in the center had rippled with water and vermilion carp. Now all was shriveled, browned and bare.

Houyi would prevail; he would come back to me, unharmed. He had never broken his word to me. And after this calamity, I would ask him to leave the army. I would not let him risk himself again; he had done enough for the kingdom. He would be mine then, freed from the cares of the realm. *I* could be stubborn, too, especially when protecting my family. If his life was the price, I did not want this fine house, our servants, and elegant courtyards. Oh, if I could have this lifetime with him, these precious decades until we were laid to rest, side by side for eternity . . . I would be content.

Tender dreams swelled through me, a brief respite from the gnawing anxiety—of us returning to the village where we first met. We would build our own house with dark-red tiles, bringing up our children in the world he had wrenched back from the sunbirds' claws, from the brink of destruction. I would mend our clothes and sew us new ones, glad to never see his gleaming armor again, which stank of iron and salt no matter how vigorously I scrubbed it. My stomach churned at the thought of the blood spilled upon it, that of my husband and his enemies. His faceless foes swarmed my mind, those felled by his blade or pierced by his arrows. Those mourned by their own parents, spouses, and children—who would curse my husband, and rejoice in his death.

I shivered, tightening my arms across my chest as a sudden chill glazed my skin. The physician warned that my moods might swing as they just did, from elation to melancholy and dread— *not* a premonition, I reminded myself fiercely as I cast such doubts from my mind.

With the blessing of the gods, Houyi would return, and nothing would part us again.

HOUYI | 后羿
THE TEN SUNS

A prequel to *Daughter of the Moon Goddess*,
reimagining the legend of Houyi and the sunbirds.

———

THE SKIES WERE AFIRE. GONE was the calm blue of day, the pale wisps of clouds drifting across the heavens. No longer did the moon and stars light the night. Our world was dying.

I glanced up, squinting as the brightness stung my eyes. The burning sky had seemed a mysterious phenomenon at first, each blazing day bleeding into the next until I was no longer sure when it had begun. Only after I had climbed the nearby peak could I make out the sunbirds frolicking above. Ten in all, their merriment rippling off them in flames. My stomach clenched with revulsion at the memory, a grotesque thing for these creatures to rejoice while causing such suffering. I had shouted at them till I was hoarse, but to no avail—which was why I had to stop them today.

As I rode upon my horse, heat flared against my face like translucent fire. Each breath seared like inhaling steam, sliding through my nostrils, down my throat. Little wonder that I encountered no living creature around; mortals, beasts, and insects sheltering wherever they could, seeking respite from this sweltering torment.

In a shady clearing, I tugged the horse's reins. As she slowed obediently to a halt, I dismounted. I ripped off my helmet, stripping away the armor from my body, the metal burning my fingers. A relief, to be clad in just my robe, though it stuck to me as sweat ran down my neck and back. I stashed the armor beneath a tree, not bothering to cover it. No thief would venture out these days, much less have the strength to lug away a pile of metal. For the enemy I faced, it would yield little protection. I would not have bothered with it except it gave Chang'e some comfort to see me clad so.

When I had bidden my wife farewell earlier, she had tried to conceal her worries—evident in the tautness of her smile, the clutch of her embrace, the too-bright sheen in her eyes. I had kissed her and held her close, feeling the thud of her heart against mine. If only I could have soothed her anxiety, but I would not relinquish my quest, not even for her. The fate of the realm rested upon my success or failure.

There was no greater honor, no more onerous duty to bear.

Despite the heat, my blood ran cold, unease thickening in my veins. But I had grown accustomed to silencing fear—a useless thing, the thief of courage and resolve. Doubt afflicts commanders as well, the difference being that we cannot show it. We dare not, if we are to lead, for who would follow a coward? How can we order another to lay down their life when we flinch from it ourselves? So, we bury it deep, and if we are fortunate, we might even trick ourselves into forgetting it exists.

But my anger? I held fast to it. The unnatural quiet, the shriveled vegetation, the dusty riverbeds without a lick of dark moisture—these fed my wrath and stiffened my resolve. Vital, as the moment neared when I must challenge a creature no mortal ever wishes to, one beloved by the gods.

We galloped over the barren land, my horse's hooves kicking

up clouds of dust. As I inhaled, it choked me—hitting the roof of my mouth, coating the back of my throat. I dug my heels into the horse's flanks, urging her onward. She did not waver though she was wearied, her movements sluggish and uncertain. Did the heat sap her strength like water from a cracked bucket? Or did she sense my own disquiet? My horse had carried me to many a battle, but none like this. This time, there was no chaos to drown my doubts, no comrades to protect, nothing to distract from what lay ahead. Just eerie silence and mounting dread in this suffocating, all-consuming heat.

Deeper in the forest, the trees offered a little shade though their leaves were sparse. We galloped through them until a mountain towered above the cracked plains, just as described in the tales. White mist shrouded its base, rising to graze the clouds that encircled the peak like a crown of smoke. At once I yanked the reins, my horse coming to a halt.

Kunlun, the elusive and legendary mountain where immortals were said to dwell when they descended to our realm. The sunbirds had not heeded my pleas before, but I would try again from this place—closer to them. Perhaps they would finally listen. I had thought Kunlun a legend told to young heroes embarking on their first adventure, to rouse their spirits with dreams of glory. It was said rare plants sprang from its soil that could whet the most jaded of appetites, that might cure fatal wounds and illnesses. Some believed that it was not only the gateway to the heavens, but to darker realms, those whose names we dared not utter. While fewer even, whispered that the secrets of eternal life were hidden there, a magical elixir to take you to the heavens. Many had sought it—both king and commoner—all had returned empty-handed, though their failures did little to dispel the rumor. It might be because we *wanted* to believe in the promise of life beyond our years. But I was not one to chase after mirages. Eternity only meant something when you had someone to share it with, not when it would take you from all you loved.

This close to Kunlun, the air cooled as though this place was shielded from the blistering heat. By the foot of the mountain, I dismounted, leading my horse toward a tall outcrop of rock flanked by trees, their leaves still green. I flung a thick blanket over the branches for a makeshift shelter, then looped the reins around a sturdy limb. Pulling out a waterskin, I poured a precious measure of water into a bowl, that my horse drank with eager, gulping sounds. She was patient; she would wait, safe in the shade of Kunlun. And if I did not return, she could yank herself free and head home.

I straightened, pushing the thought aside. Envisioning defeat was the first step toward it. Instead, I imagined my wife—the softening of her features, the light in her gaze when I returned to her in triumph. How she might trace my face with her fingers as I lifted her in my arms. And once I banished the suns, once night returned to our skies—how beautiful she would look in the moonlight, its pale rays caressing her jadelike skin.

When the king had commanded me to confront the suns, to end the suffering of the people, I had obeyed without hesitation. I was not selfless; I was doing this for myself, for my family—to save the world we lived in, the one our children would inherit. When I had weighed these fears alongside the fate of the realm, to me they were one and the same. There was nothing more worth fighting for. A comforting thought whilst danger shadowed every path on the horizon, when even victory would be tainted by threat. Come night, I would either be a charred corpse or have invoked the wrath of a god.

But I was no fool; I would try to reason with these creatures. If that failed, I might be able to scare them into leaving. A peaceable solution would be the best recourse, for I had no thirst to spill their blood; I had spilled enough.

My boots trod across the grass, soft blades of green interspersed with brittle ones of brown. Dotted among them were small flowers shaped like stars, though most had shrunken, grown as emaciated as claws. Lifting the waterskin to my lips, I took a long and reckless drink. As I closed my eyes, my heart thudded in my chest. And there was something more, that silent thrum reverberating against my body from the bow slung across my back. The silvery metal was carved with the exquisite details of a tiger, the arches from both limbs of the bow shaped like fangs. Somehow, it remained cool even after being baked in the sun—as did the pendant tucked beneath my robe, a jade disc carved with a dragon. Was it these that allowed me to venture here? Treasures from the Emperor of Heaven, gifted to his chosen warrior to save the mortals—or so I had been told by the white-haired immortal who had appeared in my dreams, bestowing these items upon me.

"Tell no one of this," the immortal had said, a faint glow emanating from his form. "It is *you* alone who must end this, else the Mortal Realm is doomed. To bring another is to sentence them to death." In his voice rang a note of command that might have chafed had it come from another. But it was not condescension or disdain, just the irrefutable note of prophecy.

I had nodded solemnly, in a daze, certain it was a dream—except I had woken with the pendant fastened around my neck, my fingers clasped around the bow. I was glad Chang'e had not seen them, that I did not need to lie to her though the concealment troubled me. Still, it was a precious solace that no matter what happened, I had the Emperor of Heaven's blessing—who was said to be benevolent, wise, and just.

At the foot of the mountain, a path wound through the cypress trees and bamboo. A welcome breeze stirred the air, laced with the scents of jasmine and sandalwood—of incense, prayers, and hope. My stride was quick but cautious, as the pathway was steep. It would be a sorry fate to slip over the edge and plummet to an inglorious end. But was there such a thing as a *good* death? All death brought pain, an abrupt ending to an unfinished story, for who could say in all honesty that their life was complete?

My mind drifted again to my wife, and I wondered what she was doing. She neither embroidered nor played an instrument. Was she reading? Resting upon our bed? I imagined her pacing the floor; she did not like to be idle. And most of all, she did not like me leaving as I had done, unsure of when I would return. I never wanted to be parted from her either. But I had said nothing, unwilling to distress her with my burdens.

Near the peak, the light was almost blinding, the skies drowned in rivers of copper. Above, the sunbirds shone as orbs of living fire, a feather of deepest crimson curling from their brows, quivering like leaping flames. As they soared through the heavens at an unearthly pace, embers trailed in their wake. Ten suns, when only one should have risen. As my eyes narrowed in fury, they swung toward me in eerie unison as though sensing my thoughts.

"Go home, mortal. This is no place for you," one of them said, its voice possessing a singsong quality to it like a child reciting a nursery rhyme.

I rose to my full height, speaking as steadily as I could. "It is *you* who must go home. You have scorched our forests, dried our rivers, and withered our crops to ash. Many mortals have already perished; countless more are suffering."

As silence descended, I began to hope they would heed my words, that perhaps they had not heard me the last time. But then the largest sunbird cocked its head and laughed. "If mortals are dying from this, you are far too feeble. *You* look well enough, with flesh on your bones and the strength to climb Kunlun."

Another swooped closer, its claws gleaming. "Do not lie to us, mortal. Kunlun below is lush and green."

I gritted my teeth, swallowing my anger. "I am more fortunate than others; I am the king's general. Kunlun may be protected from your harm—but look upon the lands beyond, see the devastation you have wreaked."

"Devastation?" one repeated in disbelief, ruffling its vermilion feathers. "Our light is a blessing. We are revered. Worshiped. Mourned, when winter shortens our flight. For too long have we been yoked to sunrise and sundown. Now we have tasted the freedom of playing together in the skies, we will never relinquish it. We will never leave; we are enjoying ourselves too much."

"You must." I spoke forcefully in the voice my soldiers feared. "You are killing our world; you are killing us all."

One of them, smaller than the rest, tilted its head. The feather on its brow glowed like metal worked in a forge. "Sisters and Brothers, maybe we should go home to Mother. She must have recovered by now. She must be worried . . . or furious."

"She will not mind," one of her siblings assured her. "She does not care for the mortals. Otherwise, she would have come to stop us before."

Was their mother the goddess of the sun? Why would she let them sow such destruction? And what might she do to me should I hurt them? No, I rebuked myself. I must not think on this. I must focus on the perils at hand, not allow new ones to spring to life.

The largest sunbird spoke now. "Little Sister, don't let this mortal frighten you. He is a fraud who spins tall tales. We have heard no cries from here."

Their insults stung, but I would not be baited. "You heard nothing because you chose not to listen. Descend closer to the earth; let your eyes and ears reveal the truth."

"A clever ruse," another scoffed, its feathers a deeper gold than the rest. "He is a fortune hunter, seeking to capture us. This is no more than a hot summer."

The others nodded eagerly, the smallest sunbird bowing her head in acquiescence.

As they shot into the skies again like the blades of a fan flared wide, the hold over my temper wavered. "You heartless creatures," I accused them in ringing tones. "I am neither a liar nor fortune hunter, but a warrior who has fought many battles, defeating monsters across our realm. Return home or I will show you no mercy." I did not know where this reckless boast came from, but I could not take it back. I dared not reveal the terror that clung to my bones like ice.

"Make us go," one jeered. "Even the Celestial Emperor dares not strike us. Neither mortal nor immortal can stop us when we are all together."

"Celestial Emperor?" I repeated in confusion. I had heard of no such monarch.

They ignored me, spiraling higher into the skies like fiery comets. In a moment they would be out of hearing. Out of reach. "Wait!" I called after them in desperation. "Why do this? Why don't you leave us in peace?"

The largest of them swung around, swooping toward me in lazy circles. Its pupils glinted wetly like newly spilled blood. "Because it *pleases* us to," it hissed. "Because we are *bored* of our duties, to light this world at dawn and depart at dusk. Because we want to be *freed* of such shackles, to play together. And most of all, because we care *nothing* for your pathetic world."

As it flapped its wings, flames surged from its feathers, scorching my robes. At once, I dropped down, rolling on the dirt to extinguish them. Their laughter rang clear, resonating between my ears. Fury seared like a fistful of coals against my chest; such lack of remorse was despicable. I shot to my feet, whipping the silver bow free and raising it high. My fingers plucked its string, curving easily in my grasp. As a translucent arrow of ice formed between my fingers, I steadied my grip. A strange pulse thrummed through my veins, sapping my strength—not in the strain of limbs but somewhere deep in my core. Drawing a long breath, I drove all distraction from my mind. The arrow sprang free, cleaving a path between the sunbirds. I had not missed; I had sought to snare their attention, not draw their blood.

"Go now, or I will strike you down the next time." My tone thickened with menace. Persuasion had not worked.

All ten sunbirds stilled, their heads swinging my way. "Mortal, how did you come by this weapon?" one of them snarled.

The Emperor of Heaven. The proud words leapt to my tongue, but I recalled the immortal's warning to say nothing. "Do you know it? Do you fear it?" I challenged instead, hoping to scare them. "I have never missed my shot. Leave now, and I will not harm you. All will be well."

Their laughter was like the jangling of brass wind chimes. As they shook their feathers, a seething shower of sparks cascaded upon me. I darted aside, just in time, before I caught fire.

"Mortal braggart." A sneer rang out. "You'll never strike us; you are too slow."

I ground my jaws together. It had been a long time since anyone dared to mock me. Something in the way they spoke reminded me of children's taunts, the bullies others steered clear of on the playground—yet their actions were beyond redemption. They would not stop, and so I would make them. Pride lifted my chin as I met those ten pairs of blazing eyes, even as my mind frantically searched for words that might soothe the roiling tension.

Before I could speak, the large one spread its wings. "Scuttle home, mortal. Irk us further, and we will hunt down your kin and scorch the flesh from their bones, then pluck their eyes from their sockets."

As the others cackled, an image of my wife slid into my mind: Chang'e in the clutches of these cruel creatures, their claws sinking into her tender flesh. Her eyes wide with horror before they were torn out. My limbs clenched with terror. Rage descended like a dense fog, a single desire hardening within to destroy these wicked creatures who threatened us all. To them, mortal lives were as dispensable as fruit plucked from a tree and tossed away after one bite.

Casting my doubts aside, I drew another arrow—letting it fly, hurtling through the nape of the sunbird, the one that had dared to threaten my beloved. It was the largest of them all; perhaps its defeat might shock the rest into retreat. I had no desire to hurt them, but I would do what I must to keep us safe. Amber drops of its blood splattered as its piercing cry wrenched the quiet, raising the hairs along the back of my neck. The creature convulsed in throes of agony, frost forming upon its body as the flames from its feathers extinguished, leaving them as dull as ash. The creature fell from the sky, not like a stone, but like a kite spiraling down on a windless morn. It slammed into the ground, its claws curled inward, its splayed wings unmoving.

Fear stabbed deep, remorse slashing my chest. With this one strike, all hopes of a peaceable solution had disintegrated. How could I have allowed its threats and mockery to get to me as though I were some untrained soldier? I had been cursed, menaced, and cajoled in battle before. But when the sunbird had threatened my family, my wife and my unborn child—something in me broke. There was no choice now but to see this to the bitter end. I must slay them all without mercy, for if not, they would hunt me down and all I loved—no longer for sport but for vengeance.

Far more vicious, infinitely deadlier.

Screeches rent the air, stabbing my ears. As one, the sunbirds plunged toward me, swifter than a gale. I dared not look away from the murderous glint in those red-ringed eyes, eighteen of them now fixed upon me.

My hands were steady despite the terror that clawed my insides, until I was raw all the way through. My fingers worked quickly, ice arrows flying free, slicing through the flames. Another fell. Then, a third, its feathers scorching my shoulder as it crashed by my feet. Blood slid over my knuckles, running down my arm. My palms were slick with it, and as for the pain—I felt nothing, my instincts binding tight the horror swelling within.

A strange exhaustion took root within my core—fatigue so heavy, it was like being entombed in stone. As a wave of fire erupted toward me, faster than I could evade it, my arrow sprang forward to take down another sunbird. I did not risk my life lightly; I would fight until my last breath. I braced for pain, for my skin to blister. Regret pulsed through me as quick as my stuttering heartbeat: to have held my wife a little longer, to have looked upon our child's face—

Flames engulfed me, ravenous and hissing. My eyes squeezed shut, stung by the smoke and glare, seeking a shard of sanity in this nightmare. As I drew in one ragged breath, then the next, it struck me . . . I was still alive. There was no agony or torment, none beyond my fatigue and bloodied hands. I forced my eyelids apart. A cool light sheathed me, rippling across my body, quenching the fire. It was as the immortal had said, the jade pendant had protected me from the sunbirds' attack.

Relief swept through me. I would not die today; I would keep my promise to my wife to return to her. A numbness took over, my hands working at a feverish pace. Arrows sprang from my fingers with renewed vigor, whistling relentlessly through the air to plunge into sunbirds. My body instinctively swerved from their attacks, the sparks that scattered like windblown pollen. As I aimed my next arrow, I stilled. Alone in the clear heavens shone a single crimson sphere.

Just one sunbird left, when there had been ten. It hovered above as though frozen by grief or terror, or both. Something yanked at my chest, a weakness that must be quashed. I could not show this creature any mercy, for vengeance must be rooted in its heart. It had watched me slay its siblings; it must hate me beyond all reason. I would not be so careless to leave this enemy alive; I would destroy it despite the pity burrowing through me.

I steeled myself, raising my bow, a shaft of ice gleaming between my fingers. My gaze narrowed until all I saw was the shining beacon of light, its pupils no longer red but as black as mine. As my wife's. As my child's would be.

"Don't kill me." Its voice cracked with emotion. "Who will light your world if you do?"

"Little Sister" the others had called her. She was the one who had tried to persuade the others to leave. But she was no less guilty than the rest, her actions speaking louder than her words. And yet, the fear thrumming in her tone and the truth in her plea halted my hand. As my rage receded, the heat dissipating from my veins, reason returned to berate me. Was I cruel enough to strike this final blow?

"How can I trust you? You will seek vengeance on me." My hands did not falter, keeping the arrow trained upon her—yet it was harder this time, a leaden weight in my chest.

"I swear to perform my duties to the mortals. To never seek revenge," she said with utter solemnity.

"I slew your siblings. All nine of them," I said, not to gloat but to test her.

A sigh unfurled from her throat like the wind rustling the leaves. "I would gladly peel your skin from your flesh and scatter your bones to the Four Seas." Her gaze radiated heat, her tone roiling with grief. "But I want to live. I want to return to my mother. I will keep my word to you."

Her vehemence was chilling, yet her honesty convinced me more than any plea or flattery. She did not seem terrifying anymore, quivering as though afraid, though her power was undoubtedly vast. Had I been wrong? Had I mistaken the sunbirds' callous youthful arrogance for pure wickedness? It did not justify their actions, and yet the possibility sickened me.

"Go," I said in a low voice. "Return home."

Not another word did she speak, spreading her wings and soaring away. The skies were no longer ablaze but a peaceful blue once more. I sucked in a breath of air and held it fast, devoid of that tinge of char, its heat blunted. I dropped the bow, falling to my knees. In the distance, cheers erupted—and borne on the wind, I caught the faint chant of my name. They must know it was my hand that brought down the sunbirds, that I had saved us all.

But where was the triumph? Why was there grief? And what would be my reckoning?

One sunbird left to light the realm. A grain of solace to her parents' void of grief. I did not delude myself; I had not been generous today. I was a thief, stealing nine times over a parent's joy. Now that I would become a father soon, I understood the devastation I had wreaked upon this family. Immortal hearts must bleed as mortal ones do. Such an offense could never be forgiven, no matter my reasons—and despite the sunbird's vow, vengeance would burn unquenched in her bloodline until I was buried in the earth, my name forgotten.

The sunbird was now a speck in the sky, the curtain of dusk following swiftly on her heels. Night would descend again, and mortals everywhere would heave sighs of relief. But as I stared at my hands wet with my own blood, the nine feathered bodies of the sunbirds strewn across the ground—I could not shrug aside the crawling unease that this was not an end but a curve in the path. And with so much to live for now, a beloved wife and a child to come—for the first time I feared the stirrings of change.

CHANG'E | 嫦娥
GODDESS OF THE MOON

A prequel to *Daughter of the Moon Goddess*,
reimagining the legend of Chang'e flying to the moon,
in the world of the Celestial Kingdom.

———

CHRYSANTHEMUMS WERE FLOWERING IN THE court-yard, their slender petals curved in rich purples, yellows, and reds. Above, the trees were losing their coats of green, donning jeweled shades of amber and garnet. A coolness infused the air, refreshing my senses. Autumn was almost upon us, my favorite time of year. Yet there was little delight in the beauty that abounded now, as I faced my husband's grim countenance.

"You must see another physician, Chang'e," he insisted, pulling his stool closer to mine.

"No, Houyi. What good will it do? I've heard enough of their dire predictions." My voice was faint, laden with fatigue. When was the last time I'd felt well?

"Then I will bring them to you." He spoke calmly despite the worry that creased his face.

An awkward silence fell between us, too often of late. Both of us searching for the words to bring the other around. Neither willing to listen.

My arms wrapped instinctively around the rounded curve of my stomach. A soft kick landed against my palm, a shiver of delight running through me—even as I dreaded what would come. Our child, our great joy, had become something ominous to be cautioned against. I was sick of the way the physicians shook their heads as they felt my pulse and examined my body. How they whispered to my husband, casting sidelong glances my way like I was some witless creature unable to handle their harsh prognosis. As if my body were not my own, that I had no part in this—even as it was *me* who bore the weight of their judgment, the dangers they prophesied with such callous ease.

The warnings had grown more dire of late: the complications of my situation, the risk that my child and I might die. And . . . I was frightened. How could I not be? Death, once a stranger, was now a constant presence in my mind. I turned aside, hiding my face from my husband's watchful stare. Ashamed to speak aloud my terrors, to confess how each diagnosis sapped the little hope I clung to. What would he understand of such despair and fears? He was a hero, the most valiant of mortals. He had faced death a hundred times and emerged the victor. His praises were written in books and sung in the teahouses. Gifts to honor him arrived in a steady stream each day, most of which he turned away whether chests of gold, jade trinkets, or rare artifacts.

He had told me once, the only treasure he'd ever wanted was for us to be a family, to be together until the end of our days. Yearning crept across my heart. Once I'd imagined this dream securely in our grasp . . . until the nightmares had begun, the fear for my child and me.

My mind shifted as though shielding itself from these thoughts that might drive me mad. There was one gift Houyi had kept—the elixir of immortality, bestowed on him by the gods for slaying the sunbirds that had been destroying our world. He'd been lauded for the victory, yet killing those birds had cost him greatly, taking something from him of immeasurable worth. He tried to conceal it, but I knew him almost as well as myself. It was no light matter to slay a divine creature, one beloved by the gods. Despite the clarity of his purpose, for what choice did he have but to kill them—my husband had changed since that day. In the weeks that followed, he seemed on edge, as though waiting for something to happen, for a price to be demanded for his actions. Yet what harm could the sunbirds do now they were dead? Just one remained, sworn to peace, my husband had claimed. No god had descended to strike my husband in retaliation, nor had any great calamity befallen him since.

Perhaps I was making too much of this, I assured myself, even as unease jostled my insides. No childbirth was without danger. Such fears were natural, to be expected—*not* a premonition. Most certainly, nothing to do with the immortal lives my husband had taken that day. He had even been rewarded by the gods.

Yet this elixir was as much a curse as a boon, the knowledge rankling even as it comforted. For if it were known what we possessed, a storm of unrest would be unleashed upon us. Kings and lords, thieves and villains, would clamor to seize it—and we would undoubtedly earn the enmity of those who failed. The emperor himself would demand its surrender, and how could we defy his command? No mortal—no matter how strong, revered, or blessed—could withstand such forces all at once. The choice that lay before us was stark in its simplicity: to consume the elixir or conceal it forever.

When Houyi had first shown it to me, I'd asked, "Will you take the elixir?" How my heart had pounded, a part of me flinching for the inevitable sorrow of parting. Who could refuse eternity? Much less he, who faced mortality every day on the battlefield, who had witnessed countless times the fragility of our lives, and how easily it might be ended through an unlucky tumble, the swift flight of an arrow, a strike of the blade.

He had shaken his head, taking my hand. "There is only enough for one. I will never leave you, my beloved."

I believed him, for I could not bear the thought of leaving him either. Only the two of us knew where the elixir was kept, tucked in a hidden compartment under our bed. We rarely spoke of it for fear of another overhearing, even in the quiet of our home. And so, the secret festered in silence, that of the jade bottle stoppered with gold. The key to eternal life, to power beyond one's dreams. A secret nestled beneath our bodies when we slept, an unseen divide between us where once there was none, a weight upon our hearts and minds—unspoken but never forgotten.

"The elixir. What shall we do with it?" I asked now, bracing myself for he did not like to speak of it. Perhaps it reminded him of what he had forsaken.

"Why are you thinking of this?" He frowned, shaking his head. "Chang'e, do not worry yourself over such things. You will not die. You will be safe and well, as will our child. We are seeing the physicians to find out as much as we can. I won't let anything happen to you." His expression hardened, turning forbidding. Another foe might have quailed and fled, yet what could frighten Death?

"Do you ever think about taking the elixir?" I repeated my question of old, refusing to be diverted. Wanting to be assured.

"Not without you. Never, without you," he said without pause.

His answer gladdened me; it should have been enough. However, my treacherous mind demanded more, wandering again to the ceaseless realm of uncertainty.

Perhaps he sensed my disquiet for he lowered his head to mine, as he murmured, "I will seek out another elixir, and then we will take it together. Would you like that, for us to live forever in the heavens?" The light in his eyes was both bright and resolute. What might be empty words from another was a pledge from him.

Forever, with the one I loved most. It seemed too much, too greedy to want such a thing. An impossible dream, but that was why dreams were often more enticing than reality.

"What if you never find a second one?" I asked.

A slow smile spread across his face. "Then we will grow old together, surrounded by our children and grandchildren. We will savor each moment of a life well spent."

Those words banished the uneasy stirrings from my heart. His hand moved to cover mine, his thumb stroking my palm with deliberate measure. A melting warmth rippled through my veins. I turned my hand over, clutching him, pulling him closer. He let himself fall toward me—I was no match for his strength should he resist—his body pressing mine with delicious weight. His lips dropped to my neck, sliding up to my cheek, tantalizingly close to my lips. My breath caught, all worry forgotten as he clasped me to him with enthralling urgency yet tenderness.

What was eternity to love? To be held by him this way, like I was the only person who mattered in the world, to feel this fullness in my chest, to have him beside me as we lay in our bed—all this was worth more than ten lifetimes.

The harsh glare of morning woke me the next day, sunlight falling upon my face. I had forgotten to close the curtains the night before. I raised myself up on an elbow, the ever-present weight of our child pressing against me. My husband was already dressed, his hair slicked into a topknot. I preferred it loose against his shoulders, or even tied partway. He looked ready for battle now, solemn and grave.

"Come, Chang'e." He held out his hand. "The physician's hall will be open soon."

"I don't want to go." While I would have usually conceded to his will in matters he felt strongly about—this was my body, my life. Our child.

He did not drop his hand. "This time will be different. We must not give up."

I bit back a refusal, resentment flickering within at how easily he disregarded my concerns. Deep in my heart something fractured, the barest crack, yet it now marred the surface of what was once whole. Why did Houyi not listen? Perhaps it was his nature, always searching for a way or an answer that pleased his ears, that aligned with his sense of rightness. Some might call it arrogance. If so, it was his due as the finest general in the realm, the great warrior who had saved the world. He was accustomed to bending fate to his whim, dragging it to heel. His resolve was one of the reasons I loved him, and also what drove me to my wit's end now.

The physician would offer the same opinion as all the ones before. I knew this as surely as I could scent rain in the air, as when I had first sensed I was with child. While I possessed neither training nor experience to guide me, this prickle of foreboding was answer enough. A helplessness engulfed me; it was too late. I was already snared in the web, despair swelling through me at the thought. Yet I bent my head in assent, sliding my hand through his. As I could no longer walk long distances in my condition, Houyi helped me into the waiting sedan chair with such gentleness, I ached within—even as a kernel of anger hardened in my chest.

SLEEP ELUDED ME THAT night. And when it finally came, it was a violent churn of terror, my insides twisting taut. I cried out as my eyes flew open. Darkness enveloped me in a suffocating sheath. My hand stretched across the bed, reaching for the comfort I already knew was not here. I was alone; Houyi had gone again to serve the king. Was it unrest by the border? A dangerous enemy, or some fearsome beast? I had forgotten the reason he was called away this time, there had been so many of late they bled into one another like paint into paper.

My fingers trailed the delicate gold chain looped around my neck, brushing the jade pendant carved with a dragon. A gift from my husband. An amulet for protection was all he had told me, reluctant to elaborate. Was it some trinket he had purchased upon a whim, swindled by some quick-talking merchant preying upon a moment of weakness? Regardless, I treasured it as I did all he had given me.

A sharp burst of pain wrenched my insides, erupting in brutal force. My hands fell to the bed, digging into the sheets as I gasped, struggling for breath. A warm wetness streaked down my legs, slippery and slick. I looked down, freezing at the sight of the dark rivulets seeping through my white robe, soaking the bedding beneath.

Terror flooded me, I could not move. Too early, it was much too early. There should be more than a month left . . . which meant my child was in danger, as was I.

Another wave of pain slammed into my body. My cry splintered into ragged moans. There was no answering shout of concern, no footsteps pounding toward me in haste. The attendants were gone for the night, and I had given our housemaid leave to visit her ailing father. Houyi would have been furious; he had ordered that I was not to be left alone. But I had thought there was time yet; I would be safe. Now I was trapped in my room, with the closest physician over half a mile away. In our large house set among these vast gardens, who would hear my cries?

I had feared death all my life, any mortal would be lying if they claimed otherwise. But this was the first time I *faced* it. If I died tonight—alone—I would not even have a chance to bid my beloved husband farewell. I was not brave or valiant as Houyi. I could not hide my feelings behind a mask of calm. I was shaking all over, my tears mingling with the sweat that slid down my face, broken gasps squeezed from my chest. Such fear filled me. Death was terrifying enough, without the added anguish of knowing it would take my child, too. I had not held or seen my child, but they were a part of me—this bond between us of flesh and blood was forged pure and unbreakable. A surge of protectiveness rose through the shuddering fear, hardening into a core of iron. A single thought surfaced with blazing clarity: I would not let my child die, not while there was another way. I would fight, for us.

Agony tore through me, sharp and merciless, snapping my resolve. My mind went blank, the pains coming swifter, the last lull barely a respite. Guttural sounds choked from my throat as a crushing sense of doom sank over me. Teeth gritted, legs stretched taut, I pounded the mattress with my fists, praying for the hurt to subside, for someone—anyone—to come to my aid.

There was only silence. I shoved myself from the bed, staggering to my feet, forcing myself to move. If I could make it to the courtyard, I might be able to draw someone's attention. Despair makes dreamers of us, yet this spark of hope pushed me onward. As I stumbled past the table, pain speared me again. My limbs buckled as I fell to the floor. My eyes darted to the bed, its crumpled sheets stained with blood—my mind whispering of what else was hidden there, beneath our bed.

The elixir. It would save us . . . the only thing in the world that could.

I shrank from the thought. The elixir wasn't mine to take. I had not killed the sunbirds; I had not earned this prize. It belonged to my husband who had turned his back on immortality because of me. I had been glad then, relieved at his decision. How could I now think of stealing it? How could I betray him? I was vile indeed to consider such a thing . . . yet how could I not, with death hovering over me?

Houyi always said one couldn't give up, I reminded myself. *When life was at stake, one should snatch at any advantage, for there was no return from death. He would want this, he always said I was more precious to him than anything in the world.*

Persuasive words, memories conveniently plucked and reshaped to soothe the rumblings of my conscience. When death was at hand, one's true character showed like a reflection in a mirror. I was a selfish coward; I did not want to die. And yet, it was not just for me but for our child. I would not let us succumb to this fate.

The pain faded, allowing a moment's lucidity. There was little time to waste. The agony would return, a relentless tempest. I pushed myself to my feet. There was a new alacrity to my movements, an invigorating rush in my veins. Somehow, I found the strength to rip away the bloodstained covers, dropping them where they pooled by my feet. With both hands I tugged at the heavy mattress, until it slid to the floor. There it was, tucked in the far corner of the bedframe, amid the carved lotuses and mandarin ducks. I ran my fingers along the wood until they felt a shift in the grain, the thinnest crack. I pulled but it did not yield. Digging my nails in, I yanked again with all my might. It gave way, a small wooden compartment coming away in my palm, containing a small bottle within. In the dark, the jade shimmered, its honeyed fragrance whispering of release from the shackles of torment.

Pain reared once more, gouging at my insides. The child stirred, kicking at the walls of my belly. Did they feel the anxiety pounding through my veins, the doubt and guilt that assailed me? Or did they sense my hesitation, and were urging me to save them? It was easier to believe the latter as I pried away the stopper from the bottle. A shimmer of gold dust wafted into the air as a rich fragrance sprang forth like I was in an orchard of peach trees. The scent streaked through my nostrils, down my throat, my mouth watering with a sudden ravenous hunger.

What about Houyi? Part of me still clung to what was right and honorable, that soundless voice within now frayed with despair. *How could you do this? Don't you love him?*

My hand stilled midway in lifting the bottle. "I do love him," I whispered aloud. "More than anyone."

Liar, my conscience chided me. *Else you wouldn't be doing what you are now.*

I should have corked the bottle, returned it to its hiding place. Replaced the covers and awaited my fate, the one the gods had marked for me. Better to face that end than spend eternity regretting my treachery, than to betray the one I loved.

But I would not.

I would do this for me. I would do this for my child. I would grasp life, plunging into unknown waters, praying I'd make it to shore. My hand was shaking as I tipped the elixir into my mouth. Warm liquid spilled onto my tongue, the acrid bitterness jolting my senses as I suppressed the instinctive urge to gag.

"I love him, I'll never love another," I whispered to myself as I placed a protective palm over my stomach. "But I choose us."

I closed my eyes and swallowed. As the last of the elixir slid down my throat, a coldness spread through me like I had fallen into snow, my pains dissipating. In its place coursed a tingling, glittering energy. I stared at my hands, catching the light gleaming through the seams at my fingertips, streaking across the lines in my palms, rippling through my veins. Such radiance flooded my vision, illuminating me from within. A glow enveloped my skin like a lantern whose candle had been lit, that of the moon emerging from behind a cloud.

My body went limp, a heartbeat before it was swung up into the air, snared by some tangling, all-encompassing force. I struggled, dread pinning me for I could no longer control my limbs, unable to wrench free of this hold.

Not this way, I thought frantically. *Not without a chance to explain or leave a letter. For my husband to return to our empty home, to wonder the worst.*

Though, what I did tonight was more terrible than anything he could have conceived.

My vision blurred, tears springing into my eyes. I groped at the air as my feet were thrust through the windows, their panels springing apart. I scrambled to find something to hold on to, my fingers clutching at the splintered frame. But I was torn away with the effortless ease of blowing the seeds from a dandelion, the stained silk of my robes twisting and fluttering in the wind.

"Chang'e!"

At his powerful cry, my heart both soared and plunged. His voice was at once so familiar and beloved—yet now it scalded my ears as I burned with shame. I was a thief caught in the act, my selfish nature laid bare. He had returned, too late. Had I been too impatient, driven mindless by fear? Or perhaps, deep down, a part of me had coveted the elixir all along.

My skin was glazed with sweat as I quenched the impulse to look away. I would return his gaze, accept any justly deserved recrimination. I hungered, too, for this last sight of him—standing by the window, his armor gleaming by the light of the heavens. His head was bare, his black hair coiled into a topknot. Eyes wide with shock, sorrow mirrored in their dark pupils. And a flicker of something else—was it disappointment, or even . . .

hate? As his hand stretched toward me, a new pain impaled my heart, one that left wounds unseen, those that would never heal.

His eyes narrowed, his mouth thinned as he raised his bow. Was he furious enough to shoot me? But then he lowered his weapon almost at once. I cried out his name, a plea for forgiveness—yet he could not hear me, my sobs swallowed by the howling wind. The child within kicked as though sharing my despair. I clasped my hands over my stomach in a vain attempt to soothe them. A strange energy thrummed through my blood, yielding a new strength. My aches and pains, all that was flawed and broken in my mortal state was gone like snow covering the muddied earth, water smoothing the pitted sands. Yet there was no joy or relief, just the bitterest of remorse.

I stared at my husband, until—at last—he vanished from sight. Grief seared me for what we had lost, my betrayal sliding between my ribs like a knife. As tears streamed down my face, I forced myself to turn from my home . . . for it was mine no more.

I was no longer mortal.

My heart did not lighten, sunken beneath a new burden, one that formed the moment I took the elixir. Yet my child and I were safe—at least, for now. I could not regret this choice, no matter the cost. I still had our child to whom I would be as father and mother. And as I gazed into the horizon aglitter with stars, incandescent with the light of the moon, so full and perfect tonight—I vowed to make a new life for us, wherever we were. This would not be the end of our story, we would survive—and together, we would face what would come.

HOW CLEARLY, I REMEMBERED my ascent to the skies. After all, I have relived this every day since I came here, since I became immortal. The mortals worshiped me though I did nothing to deserve it. On the fifteenth day of the eighth lunar month, they laid out their offerings, murmuring prayers over the fragrant incense smoke that spiraled to the heavens. The Moon Goddess, they called me, but was there ever a goddess as powerless?

When the mortals sang songs to me, I wondered what they truly thought. Many believed I had betrayed my husband. Some imagined me as the unworthy wife to a hero, thinking Houyi deserved better. How I missed him. A ruthless warrior and yet, a tender and loving husband. He would have been a good father to our daughter, a girl who possessed his fierce spirit—to our other children, perhaps those who might have taken after me instead. Children who were lost to us in this lifetime. Children we would never have. My heart curled with a familiar ache. I welcomed it, a relentless reminder that I had not forgotten him.

Immortality was a hollow gift, regret poor company for a broken heart. Yet I cannot curse the elixir that saved me, for it had saved our daughter, too—Xingyin, named for the stars in the sky, the eternal companion to the moon.

If the mortals doubted my honor in silence, Their Celestial Majesties denounced me as scheming, selfish, treacherous—unworthy of immortality. This remote place they exiled me to was a wilderness to them, the one accidental act of benevolence bestowed upon me. I did not like being bound here, but I was grateful to find wonder and beauty in this place, to have Ping'er by my side—more a friend than an attendant. She stayed with me willingly when few would have wanted to serve a disgraced mistress. There was even solace in my endless task of lighting the lanterns, a way to silence my mind, to relive the memories I never wanted to forget. I did not complain about my punishment. I accepted it readily . . . and there were days I felt I deserved worse.

Each night, I performed my tasks with diligence, until my arms and back ached and my fingers were blackened with soot. The nights of the full moon were the hardest; one thousand lanterns in all needed to be lit. Ping'er had offered to teach me what magic she knew, but I had no talent in it. Attempting to channel my powers plunged me into such exhaustion, it seemed a futile exercise. What need was there for magic? I had lived long enough without it. While it might hasten my task, time knew no bounds here. It was a fitting part of my punishment to be a powerless goddess. Magic would only remind me of what I had become, all I had lost the day I became immortal. Let this onerous duty be part of my penance, I accepted it wholeheartedly.

Yet life would not be all misery and grief. I had my daughter, someone to care for, to return to after my labors. In the echoes of her smile I found love again, hope reborn in the brightness of her eyes. No, I had not chosen wrong. We were alive, we had defied our destiny.

And as long as we lived, there would be hope . . . that I might see my husband again.

TWILIGHT

LIWEI | 力伟
THE SNOW GINSENG ROOT

A tale of *Daughter of the Moon Goddess*,
in which Liwei and Xingyin seek out the snow ginseng root.

———

NIGHT HAD FADED, THE DAWN streaked with ash and rose. The lanterns were still lit as I strode toward Xingyin's chamber. I knocked upon the door firmly, my guilt at waking her vanishing when a curse from within broke the silence. I grinned, imagining her scowl, part of me relishing her ire.

"What is it, Liwei? It's still dark. Can't it wait?"

"No. You shouldn't sleep until noon, anyway," I replied unsympathetically.

"Just once," she said with feeling, her voice muffled through the wood, "I would like to sleep till noon."

Life in the palace began early each day, whether for an attendant or the emperor. It had been so since I was a child, each waking hour filled with lessons, the tutors and subjects changing over time, though the schedule remained fixed. My mother told me it was training for when I took the throne, and I was glad to now have a companion—a friend—in Xingyin. Our mornings were spent studying in the Chamber of Reflection, while afternoons found us on the field with the soldiers, training in sword fighting and archery. This was where Xingyin had first learned to shoot, and she had outpaced me soon after. Any blow to my pride was outweighed by the joy of watching a friend rise, to accomplish what lay in their blood. Our days were full, yet most evenings she would remain in my room after our meal, even when I'd curbed my selfish impulse to ask her to stay. During the nights when she sensed I was troubled, she would play a song on her flute, better than any of the trained musicians at court. But the times I most cherished were when she just sat there, reading or conversing with me. Such simple things lent a semblance of normality to our relationship, and I hoped it would never change.

How quiet my days had been before she came into my life. It was why I had begun painting as a way to fill the void. In Xingyin, I'd inadvertently found my favorite subject—yet I rarely allowed myself the indulgence of painting her, for she already lingered far too long in my mind.

When had it begun, this ceaseless desire to be close to her? I had always enjoyed her company, right from our first encounter. Her candor and wit amused me, coupled with her generous yet stubborn heart. She possessed the skill of a warrior along with the mind of a scholar, and her magic was as fierce as her ambition—though I was unsure what drove her when she cared little for position or title.

Lately, I'd found myself devising excuses to keep her with me longer in the evenings, the rare time that belonged to us alone. My pleasure in her company began to give way to a more unsettling emotion, a desire for *more*. It would be dangerous should another discern it. If others knew of our connection, they would seek to use it, to control her. I could not thrust her into the den of snakes that was the Celestial Court, not until I could ensure her safety.

While my position conferred great privileges, these came with tethers of their own. Unlike most, my life was not an uncharted sea. I knew my place in this realm and the path I would take. My days, since childhood, were spent in training for the role I would fulfill—to ascend the throne, rule the kingdom, marry someone who would grace the crown. There was already much discussion at court regarding the search for a suitable candidate. An unwelcome thought, for my parents had wed in such an alliance and found little joy in their union. But I would not shirk my duty. There was no place for love when a kingdom was at stake . . . unless one was prepared to relinquish it. My heart was not mine to give; I must guard myself better, keep my distance from Xingyin, though it was becoming harder to stay away. I could not allow myself to slip again as I had in the Celestial market, imagining a carefree life that could never be. A weight sank over me, as my thumb stroked the Sky Drop Tassel by my waist. A gift of friendship, I reminded myself, for that was all we could ever be.

Moreover, Xingyin would not be content to remain here, nor should I attempt to keep her in this gilded cage. She should make her own life, not shape herself to mine, entangled by the cords that bound me. In the Courtyard of Eternal Tranquility, we were shielded from the cares of the Celestial Court, but that would not last. Once I assumed my duties, our peace would disintegrate; we would be plunged into scrutiny both malicious and unkind. The court would dislike her—someone they could neither read nor use, who would not cave to their demands. And if they could not change her . . . they would break her. As an uneasiness stirred, I cast aside these fears of an uncertain future. What mattered was the present.

Filled with sudden urgency, I rapped the door again. "We must leave before the sun rises," I told her, leaning against the door as I prepared for an argument.

The door was thrown open. Losing my balance, I lurched forward, gripping the wooden frame as I stumbled into the room. Despite my years of training, she still caught me off guard with ease—which pleased me more than it irked. She stood over me as I straightened, grasping at my scattered dignity.

"Liwei, what's so important that I had to see it before sunrise?" Her smile was a little smug, like she relished making me fall.

"Don't you want to get out of the palace?" I countered, knowing her preference.

Her eyes shone brighter than the lanterns outside. "Next time, *Your Highness*," she said teasingly, "you should lead with that invitation to gain a warmer reception."

"How warm?" I found myself asking, against caution and all sense.

Her cheeks flushed, as she folded her arms over her chest. "Perhaps you would not have found yourself tumbling through the doorway."

I let the moment pass; it was more prudent to not press. "Was that intentional?" I asked instead.

"Of course." She angled her head up, her mouth curving wider. "I was waiting till the door creaked beneath your weight."

We left the courtyard then, the rhythmic rumble of the waterfall smothering our footsteps. The attendants would awaken soon but we would return before we were missed, in time for our morning class.

"Where are we going?" she asked, as we crossed the gardens of the Inner Court.

"Have you been to Crystal Snow Mountain?"

"I've only been to the places you've taken me to." Her teeth sank into her lip as though trying to bite back those words.

"Where were you before?" I asked, despite knowing she was reluctant to speak of her past. Whatever happened had hurt her deeply, its wounds still raw.

"Far from here. It was isolated. Small. You would not have gone there."

The halting way she spoke stirred my emotions. It was tempting to sweep aside the remaining barriers, to ask for her trust and the responsibility it would entail. But I did not, afraid of what she might divulge, of how it might change things. What if it drove a wedge between us? What if I was forced to send her away? I would rather wait until she was ready to share her secrets, or until I could better safeguard her from any threat.

"Where is this mountain?" she asked.

"Close to the shores of the Northern Sea. It's not far."

"The Northern Sea?" She frowned. "Did they not aid the Demons in the war?"

"We're on civil terms with them now. Moreover, we won't be trespassing into their domain; the mountain lies within Celestial territory," I assured her.

We entered a deserted courtyard by the outer walls of the palace, the one we'd used before to leave unseen. Here, the grass brushed our knees, the pavilion roof was weathered, its wooden pillars pitted and worn—an unusual sight when everything else in the palace was so immaculately tended. Yet it was better for us that it remained forgotten. Xingyin stood still as I cast the enchantment to shield our auras, summoning a wind to bear us over the wall—upon a waiting cloud. As we flew into the sky, the first shafts of the morning sun fell over us with a gentle warmth. Calm filled me, yet I had never felt so alive.

"Why did you want to go to the mountain today?" she asked.

"Today is the summer solstice in the Mortal Realm, when the snow ginseng berries ripen. While the ginseng itself is a sacred plant that cannot be harvested, its berries and seeds are given freely for planting." My gaze slid to hers. "If you'd paid more attention in class, you would know this."

She wrinkled her nose. Our tutor in herbology was not a favorite of hers. He was stern and arrogant, nor had he ever forgiven her for almost falling asleep during his first class.

"These are important lessons, even though the subject may not seem as interesting or exciting as General Jianyun's," I reminded her. "Nature is everywhere. With it, we are never wholly defenseless. You might lose your weapon in battle, an enemy might seize it from you, but you can always find a useful plant if you know what you're looking for."

She grinned. "What if you pluck the wrong herb? One that strengthens instead of weakens your foe?"

"That is why we study," I reminded her pointedly.

"What is special about the snow ginseng root? Does it grant some great power? Strengthen one's lifeforce?"

"It has a potent effect on soothing one's mind and spirit. A useful aid to meditation."

She glanced at me. "Why would you want this?"

I did not. This excursion was not about the root, but the desire to see more of the realm with her, an excuse to leave the palace. "My parents like to collect rare items. It might be useful one day" was what I said instead.

She nodded somberly. "Your mother might find such an item of particular use."

I cleared my throat, burying a laugh. My mother's temper was renowned and, unfortunately, Xingyin had borne the brunt of it more than once. "I will be sure to offer the ginseng root to her once it has matured."

She raised her face, basking in the warmth of the sun. "I am glad to be out. We hear of so many wondrous places, I want to see as many as I can."

"What is the point of life, if not to live it?" I agreed. "And there is no better moment than the present, while my time is my own."

She swung to me, seemingly startled. "What do you mean?"

"Once I come of age, I will assume my official responsibilities. I will have to attend court." I spoke reluctantly, not wanting to think about our time together ending. If I no longer attended the classes, there would be no need for a study companion. While I could find another place for her, even if I had to create one—these carefree days would be a remnant of the past.

"At least, I'll be able to leave the palace at will, without the need for subterfuge," I added.

"As long as the guards don't report your whereabouts to your parents," she said with a smile.

I grinned. "We'll just have to bribe them better."

In the horizon, the waters of the Northern Sea rippled in shades of aquamarine. Our cloud swerved upward, soaring higher—the air turning colder as a snow-covered mountain loomed before us. We flew toward it, landing at the peak. All was white and silver, even the grass seemed frosted over. A stream cut across the plain, its waters possessed of an iridescent sheen. Just a short distance away was a crystal dais, upon which a plant grew, its leaves spread wide like a fan. Clusters of berries sprouted from its center, gleaming like rubies.

"Xingyin, be careful. We must only pluck the berries. Don't touch anything else, not even the leaves, else the plant will think it's being threatened," I warned.

"*Think?*" she repeated, her voice lifting in doubt.

"This plant is one of the great ancients, older than the kingdom itself. While it may not think the same way as us, its instincts are honed to precision. It could kill us with ease, should we give it cause." My eyes narrowed. "Did you listen to *anything* in that class?"

"Nothing whatsoever," she declared, raising her hands. "Though I promise to start."

The wind leapt, blowing loose strands of hair across her cheek. My hand reached out to brush them away, but I forced it down, stepping from the cloud abruptly.

As we headed toward the dais, she kept pace beside me with her long strides. Bending to inspect the ginseng, she gestured for me to come closer. I moved toward her, careful to maintain a discreet distance. Part of me wanted to touch her hand, to feel the warmth of her skin, yet my guard was up. I shifted my attention to the plant instead, the alleged reason for our excursion. The soil here was formed of shining grains, almost translucent. Silken tendrils sprang from the ginseng's plump stem, gleaming like they were spun from silver.

"The root only glows like this when its berries ripen," I told her.

"It's beautiful. Perhaps we can grow one just like it."

"Unlikely. This is the only root of its kind. Its offspring will possess strong magical properties, but the core of its power lies with the parent."

"Is it dangerous?" she asked. "If it falls into the wrong hands?"

"It guards itself well. Besides, its power is not the type that will raise or destroy kingdoms; there is no reason to covet it other than for its beauty and healing properties. It would be wicked, indeed, to harm something that only offers joy and peace to others."

"Unkindness often has no reason," she murmured. Before I could ask her meaning, she glanced at the sky, now a bright blue. "We should return soon. Our first class is with General Jianyun and he will not tolerate lateness."

I nodded, reaching for a cluster of berries—just as she did. Our hands collided, heat flaring across my skin. As we broke apart, her face reddened. I rebuked myself for such foolishness. Why did her touch affect me now, when it never had before? Steadying myself, I stretched out again to pluck a berry. It fell away in my hand, searing cold. My fingers trembled, brushing against a leaf—

Thorns erupted from the stem of the plant, sprouting like silver pins. The ground shook beneath our feet as light surged from the dais—a moment before the ginseng root swelled, its tendrils thickening as they burst through the earth, grown monstrous like the tentacles of some great sea creature. The blades of grass around us sprang up like tips of daggers, impossible to cross.

"We must flee. Summon a cloud!" Xingyin's voice was firm yet urgent, her gaze sweeping over the perils that encircled us.

Cloud summoning was something she was still learning, one of the few things that came slower to her because of her initial fears. My energy flowed to seize a cloud from the heavens, imbuing it with magic. As we scrambled upon it, a tendril from the ginseng lashed at us, its thorns scraping my sleeve, digging into my flesh. Another whipped across Xingyin's face, drawing a thin trail of blood. I cursed, but she did not flinch. Raising her hand, the lights of her energy scattered like rain, forming an enchantment.

A wind roared to life, fiercer than any I might have conjured. As it bore us higher, another thick tendril of the plant sprang up, winding around my ankle. Thorns pierced my skin, scratching my leg. I pushed the pain from my mind, flames streaming from my hands to burn it away—even as Xingyin moved swiftly, a dagger in her hand. She slashed at the root with deft strokes, cutting it apart. The hard light in her eyes was the same intense expression as when she let an arrow fly.

"Are you hurt, Liwei?" She bent to inspect my arm, using her sleeve to clean my wound, even as blood trickled down her cut cheek.

I did not reply, raising my fingers to her face. My magic flowed into her, knitting the torn flesh together seamlessly. We were fortunate to have suffered no more than these scrapes, but the incident had left me shaken.

"I was careless. I did not mean for this to happen." A clumsy apology, if it could be called one at all. It was not something I was accustomed to offering.

As she smiled at me, my heart quickened. "I thought you intended this as our morning exercise."

"Perhaps next time."

"Next time I might not get out of bed," she warned, turning to examine the devastation we'd left on the mountain. "Did we damage the root? I had to cut its tendrils to escape."

"Are you concerned for it after it tried to flay us?" I asked, partly in disbelief.

"It did not ask for our presence, nor the chaos we caused," she replied gravely.

"The core of the ginseng remains unharmed. If injured in any way, it can heal itself," I assured her.

Her expression lightened. "Shall we plant the seed tomorrow?"

"You may have the honor," I offered.

"The only honor I want is to sleep in."

She yawned, covering her mouth, and despite everything we'd just encountered, her heavy-lidded eyes stirred an unfamiliar heat inside me. Did she look this way when she awoke in the morning, my treacherous mind wondered. A dangerous thought—forbidden—that perhaps one day I would see her waking beside me, disheveled, with this very expression on her face. As my chest twinged, I turned away.

"After today, *you* should be the one to get your hands soiled," Xingyin said, with a laugh. "Let's hope the one we plant has a more placid disposition than its parent."

I laughed along with her, the strange tension within me dissipating. She evoked such conflicting emotions in me; I wanted to shield her, and yet felt safer when she was near. As I gazed into her upturned face, the remaining barriers around my heart fell away, the part of me I had always held back.

I would never forget my duty, but why should I ignore my heart? There was little use in denying these feelings; they were a part of me, too. To ignore their existence, to obscure and suppress them, might be the greater loss. The future was rife with possibilities: Perhaps Xingyin might grow accustomed to life in the palace, or I might be able to choose my own future? Perhaps these emotions would fade of their own accord?

For now, I would let the current bear me down a new path, to yield to these awakening sensations. I would reach for the joy before me, keep it close—for each moment was precious, a rare enchantment in itself, and as powerful as any magic.

WENZHI | 文智
BATTLE WITH THE BONE DEVIL

A tale of *Daughter of the Moon Goddess*,
in which Celestial soldiers fight a fearsome monster.

———

T
HE LAKE WAS ENCIRCLED BY ancient pine trees. They
reminded me of my home in the Cloud Wall—my
courtyard, always fragrant with their woody scent. Except here, the rust-colored bark was veined in gray like a web of
shadow had been strewn across it. Their feathery needles glinted
as though tipped in iron, clinking ominously as the wind blew.

Unease darted across the back of my neck before it was
swiftly extinguished. The futility of fear lay in slowing the hand
and dulling the mind, when one needed them most. I was accustomed to numbing myself to it, to give it no place—as I'd courted
danger for as long as I'd wielded a sword. It did not matter what
form an enemy took, they wanted the same thing: their victory
in exchange for my defeat. I would deny them all. To some it was
a game, a toss of the coin—but in my childhood, one slip could
mean death. There was little room for error, for misplaced trust
and flawed judgment, though it had not deterred me from enter-
ing the fray.

If one did not play, one could never win.

Despite my achievements, there was little joy in what I did. It was easy to forget the beauty in the realm, its wonder, when one was mired in despair and death. But I would not falter now, when the end was in sight—everything I had planned and striven for all these years. There would be time enough for the pleasures of the world when I had secured my place in it, along with the safety of those who relied upon me.

"Is this the Bone Devil's hideout?"

Xingyin's voice broke through my thoughts. She stood beside me, her dark eyes moving from side to side, assessing the terrain. There was no trace of anxiety, her spirit as steady as her aim. We were alike that way, holding our ground, making our way without need of another—it was one of the reasons I trusted her. While she bore secrets of her own, they did not overly concern me for her honor shone clear.

Unlike yours, my conscience whispered before I silenced it.

"The bodies were found not far from here, drained of their lifeforce and blood. One of the victims was still alive when our scouts found him," I recounted. "The creature is hungry, after being imprisoned for so long."

She frowned. "How did it escape? I thought Celestial prisons were impenetrable. Impossible to break out from."

"They are. The worst Celestial prisons are windowless pits of hell. Most prisoners lose their minds after a few decades. Each is held captive in a unique way, fashioned for them alone, in the most torturous of binds." I spoke slowly, wanting the words to sink in.

Her lips curled with revulsion. "Even monsters deserve mercy."

Even Demons, I wanted to say. I'd told her this story in part calculation, to show her the Celestials' hands were not as pristine as they wanted the rest of the realm to believe. They could be cruel, too, except they concealed it better, shaping the truth to favor them alone.

"The Bone Devil meditated for centuries to strengthen its power. It possessed a secret trait that we discovered too late—that once it advanced to the next stage of its magic, it could morph into a new form, one that rendered its existing binds useless."

She frowned. "Is the creature more powerful than when it was first captured?"

"Unfortunately, yes." I raised my voice so the others would hear. "The Bone Devil cannot be allowed to escape again. It is out for vengeance, viciously killing all who cross its path. Its magic is strong, as is its physical form, and it moves like the wind. A single puncture from its fangs and claws will inflict grave injuries."

"How many victims did it claim this time?" Xingyin sounded tense, bracing for the worst.

"Five. Two were children." Anger seethed in my gut at the creature's wickedness. Death was a soldier's shadow, but the slaughter of innocents sickened me still.

Her mouth thinned. "It will pay."

"We will make sure of it." I nodded toward the tallest of the six soldiers, the one who stood closest to me. "Soldier Yang, stay here with the others and take the lead. Weave your wards around the lake. The Bone Devil does not like water for it obscures its senses, and this will help conceal our magic once we lure it here. Stay hidden, until commanded otherwise, and hold your shields firmly so the creature cannot escape."

The soldier bowed, though a frown marred his seeming compliance.

"Speak freely, Soldier Yang," I told him.

"Why must we stay hidden?" he blurted.

"If the Bone Devil can't see you, it can't attack you. The wards will be safe."

The soldier's frown deepened when another, more battle weary, might have rejoiced. "But if we stay hidden, how will we kill it?"

"That falls to the First Archer and me." I inclined my head toward Xingyin.

As the soldier glanced at her, his lips pursed in seeming disdain. My jaw tightened as I fought back the protectiveness that had risen in me since Xingyin's near death at the hands of Governor Renyu. The memory seared, it always did—and how I wished I'd killed him that day. It had taken every bit of my willpower not to strike the final blow. When I had returned to the tent to find her on the brink of death—yet not a victim, for she was never one—something in me had snapped. A primal urge reared, to destroy the one who had hurt her. The emotion evoked had been so strong, it disconcerted me. I had always respected her skill and intelligence, even as I found myself intrigued by her. The more time I spent with her, the stronger the sensation grew, awakening new and inconvenient ones: the reluctance at having to deceive her, resentment when sadness clouded her face for I knew she was thinking of the Celestial who had broken her heart. A twinge in my chest when she yielded one of her rare smiles.

I did not like this. Emotions were unpredictable—perilous, in my situation. Xingyin might despise me if she knew the truth of my heritage. While she did not seem blindly loyal to the Celestial Kingdom, she would not look lightly upon my deceit and the role I had to play here. My instincts cautioned me to wait, to learn what she was concealing—I knew the signs having studied them myself. While I was curious, it would change nothing about my regard for her. She would have my support.

Until then, I would keep my silence. I would not jeopardize all I had fought for, no matter the temptation. I would bide my time, earn her trust. She might rage upon learning the truth—but over time, she would understand. Our connection went deeper than such matters. I had not lied about my background; rather, I'd omitted certain facts. With her, I had always been my true self. I would not willingly deceive her about who I really was, not in the way that mattered. For we were cut of the same cloth, of the same stubborn and unflinching nature—and we would either soar together or destroy each other.

Never the latter, I swore, for I would win her to my side.

Not just because she would be a useful pawn or powerful ally, although there was truth in both. In the beginning, I'd wanted to keep her close for those reasons, after witnessing her unexpected bond with the Jade Dragon Bow. If I delivered both the legendary weapon and its wielder to my father, I would earn his favor, securing my place as his heir. Only then would my mother and those under my protection be safe, for my accursed brother would no longer be able to threaten them.

This was what I had worked so hard toward, I could not rest till I had achieved it. But while my ambition remained the same, my path had shifted. The thought of my father using Xingyin for his own ends repelled me. Despite her innate strength, her refusal would not matter for he could bend her mind, manipulate her to do his bidding. Few could match his skill in those arts. My stomach turned, not just because of my inherent distaste for this use of our magic, but because deep down, I did not want her to change . . . even if it meant she would be mine.

I wanted her to remain who she was, to come to me of her own will. It would be meaningless otherwise. I resolved then to never tell Father of her gift, to keep her and her secret safe. And if it came down to it, I would fight to protect her.

Soldier Yang cleared his throat now, likely emboldened by my silence. "The Bone Devil is dangerous. Perhaps another might accompany you?"

I reined in my annoyance. The soldier was new; I should not intimidate him. He was still eager for glory, impatient for fame. Likely he imagined that I was playing favorites, allowing the First Archer the choicest part of the assignment—though it wouldn't take long for the tarnish to set in, for him to sigh with relief rather than envy those chosen for the front line. Xingyin might not appear dangerous at first, but only to the fools or untrained. Any formidable warrior could discern the intensity in her gaze, the deadly grace of her movements, the power with which she wielded her weapon. Watching her fight stirred something in me, just as when I'd first seen her shoot down General Jianyun's targets: Admiration. Respect. And an inexplicable, infuriating, sense of wonder.

I never thought anyone could capture my attention the way she had. I had hoped it was a brief fascination, as a child with a new toy, but it deepened along with our acquaintance. She had proven me wrong again and again, and I was beginning to thrive on the challenge.

I glanced at her, trying to read her expression. The soldier was both right and wrong; I *did* favor Xingyin's company above all others, though she had more than earned her position through merit. Yet a good commander did not demand blind obedience. Far better to earn it, to encourage questioning, to teach the soldiers to think for themselves and guard against every eventuality.

"All of you must remain here because we are laying a trap to lure the Bone Devil to the lake, so we can fight it together," I said to the soldiers. "Just the First Archer will accompany me to seek out the creature, as speed will be essential rather than numbers. If our group is too large, the monster will not approach. It is cowardly at heart, only attacking when it knows it can prevail— seeking victims, not a fair fight."

"Yes, Captain," they intoned as they bowed, before taking their assigned positions.

Xingyin and I left the lake then, heading deeper into the forest. After a short distance, she turned to me. "Wenzhi, should we disguise our armor? It might rouse the Bone Devil's suspicions."

Warmth flashed through me at her informal use of my name. Alone, we dispensed with the formalities that she was careful to maintain before others. I was glad to not have used a false name, for it would have deprived me of this pleasure.

I stopped by a grove of bamboo, their yellowing stalks thickly clustered. "You are right. We will change now." The urge to tease her unfolded, a frivolity I usually disdained. "Will you help me?"

A shadow fell across her face. I cursed myself for the unthinking words, evoking memories of the Celestial Crown Prince she had served. She had been his companion, but it was plain to all that their relationship went deeper. However, that was in the past—he had hurt her, and she was with me now.

"Does my request make you nervous?" A challenge was the best way to provoke her, to rouse her from sorrow or regret.

She stiffened, but instead of shying away, she stepped closer and tapped my chest, her nail clinking against my armor. Something sparked in my veins, my mouth going dry.

"Why would I be nervous?" Her eyes were alight with sudden humor. "If you need help to undress like a child, I would be willing to aid you."

I scowled at her insult, yet admired how she had spun things around with ruthless competence.

"What's the matter, Captain?" Her smile widened; she was laughing at *me* now. "Changed your mind?"

I wanted to toss caution to the wind and accept her offer, though it had been made in jest. We were on the brink of flirtation, a dance we'd sometimes engaged in since the Eastern Sea—yet never slipping over the edge. She was so rarely in this mood, a reckless part of me wanted to press onward, to see how far this game might be played. My chest constricted with an anticipation that I restrained. We were here for a purpose; if we did not find the Bone Devil soon, it would strike again.

"An illusion will suffice," I told her, releasing my magic that glittered as it glided over us.

Our armor shimmered, shifting into robes. Her hair was gathered into coils, flower-shaped pins tucked between their dark strands. Her bow morphed into a fan, my sword into a jade walking staff.

"Will this be enough?" she asked, touching the intricate embroidery on her gown. When had I imagined such details?

"It will. Our appearance is just to bait the Bone Devil, to make us seem easy prey. When it attacks, we'll need our armor and weapons on hand." I spoke somberly, even as I drank in the sight of her in these garments. The green suited her well, bringing out the color in her skin, the darkness of her hair and eyes. The last time we had dressed in such finery was for the banquet in the Eastern Sea. A night of many beginnings.

She tilted her head back. "We can't let the creature get too close, otherwise it might sense the illusion. Once we're spotted, we must quickly draw it to the lake."

As I nodded, her gaze flicked up to mine. I held it. A beat pulsed through us, her chest rising and falling with greater force. For a moment, we seemed lost in an illusion of our own, in which we were different people—not here to slay a monster but simply enjoying each other's company. An ache pulsed that this was not our reality, even as I began to hope it might be—one day, far from here. When we were no longer part of the Celestial Army, I would share with her all I was. For now, I would wait. *When* a battle was fought was often a crucial element of its outcome. Part of her heart still belonged to the Celestial Prince, and I would pry it free for I wanted it all.

Are you worthy of her? my conscience demanded.

Perhaps not, I conceded darkly. *But I will be.*

"Come, Wenzhi." She was already moving ahead of me. "We must not delay. It will be harder to fight the creature in the dark."

Deeper in the forest, the trees loomed higher, their branches weaving above until just the barest scraps of sky remained. Sunlight filtered through in thin shafts, watery and weak. The ground was barren, the atmosphere heavy, without even the lilt of a bird to lift the gloom. Had they all been scared away? Devoured? Our approach was deliberately careless, treading over crackling twigs, our hands and elbows jostling the leaves. Xingyin stumbled over a loose rock, letting out a small cry as I caught her arm. Was it an act to trick our foe, or clumsiness? I could not tell, my senses dulled when it came to her, perhaps because my emotions were entangled.

As she stiffened in my hold, I released her. She was unused to my touch, just as I rarely touched another. Both of us were guarded and I wondered yet again, what she was wary of.

"A good performance." I grinned. "You've made enough noise for every monster in these woods to hear us."

She laughed. "I'm not as cunning as that. I did trip for real, but the next one can be feigned."

I bent my head toward her. "What shall we talk about now?"

"Must we talk at all, Wenzhi?" She was adept at evading such questions.

"Yes. If we're to give the appearance of being intimate."

She inhaled sharply. "Why must it be so? Why can't we be friends out for a walk?"

"Why would friends come to this secluded forest, braving the warnings, unless they wanted to be alone?" I replied evenly.

Her eyes narrowed. "Perhaps you should have come here with Soldier Yang. He might be more inclined to play this part with you."

"He might be better company, but he doesn't shoot half as well."

"I might miss and hit you instead," she said cuttingly.

"By accident or design?"

"It depends on how much you continue to bait me."

"Are you aware of the punishment in the Celestial Army for intentionally injuring your commander?" I tried to keep a stern expression as she glared at me, undaunted.

"Then it's fortunate I am not officially part of the army." She shook her head. "Rest assured I'd never shoot a friend, whether by accident or design."

"A *friend*?" I suppressed the urge to frown. "Is that what I am?"

"Of course," she replied without hesitation. "What would you be if not, Captain?"

Her use of my title silenced me. I wanted to say more, to lift her face to mine—to ask for her heart, as I was in danger of losing mine. But this was no time for rash declarations. I would not risk everything I had set in place, the years of feigned servitude to a cause I despised. Nor would I stain her earned reputation with malicious talk of favoritism, for success undoubtedly invited envy. There were enough whispers surrounding us; I would give the gossips no more fodder. I'd wait until we were free of the Celestial Kingdom, of these positions that neither of us cared much for.

I stilled then, at the same moment she did. A scent slithered through the air, melding with the cold—of mint and cloves—so sharp, it hit the back of my throat, infusing my senses with dread.

Her voice dipped, soft yet clear. "It's near."

The creature's aura flitted closer. The wind roiled with greater force, the rustling of pine needles hardening to jangles of metal. Trees bent until they seemed entwined, locked in an unnatural embrace. At once, I tightened my hold over the illusion that clad our forms.

A silvery blur darted between the trees. At my nod, Xingyin and I dashed away, through the forest—ducking beneath the low branches, leaping over the undulating roots that seemed to rise higher with each step. Shadows stretched like inkblots, as though the last remnant of sky had been blocked from above. A coldness spiked from behind, a shudder running down my spine. Water was one of my Talents, yet the chill that emanated from this creature reached bone deep. Xingyin kept pace with me effort-lessly, her labored breathing the only sign of strain.

A white arm lashed out by the side of my face, claws glinting. Instinctively I ducked, swinging my sword—still disguised as a staff—to bat it aside. As a fleshy hand snaked around Xingyin's wrist, fury shot through me. I grabbed her arm to steady her as she staggered to a halt—yet she wrenched free of my grip, un-willing to slow me down. As she struggled to tear herself from the creature's grasp, I reached for my magic, yet flames were already coursing from her palm to strike the Bone Devil. Even now, she did not drop the act, reining in her powers—fighting back just enough to break free, but not to scare off the creature. As it fell back, we raced onward until the waters of the lake gleamed before us. Our soldiers were nowhere in sight, obeying my command to secure this place, their wards encircling it like an invisible wall. As we dashed through the barrier, I tested their strength. Soldier Yang and the others had done well. The wards were strong, crafted to allow entry yet prevent escape—though it remained to be seen whether they would hold.

Xingyin and I stopped by the shore, swinging around. The Bone Devil towered over us, its long arms springing from its torso. Silver horns arched from its head, the thick strands of its hair curling like serpents. Its flawless skin was like silk pulled taut, its eyes luminous, the tips of its claws crusted with dark stains. Remains of its past victim? It would be the creature's last.

"Come to me." A gentle yet insidious whisper.

My limbs twitched against my will. Its voice possessed an uncommon quality that drew me to it. From the confusion on her face, Xingyin was struggling, too. This was not compulsion, but more like a lure that called to our bodies instead of our minds.

"Shield yourself," I hissed between clenched teeth. At once her energy surged, forming a barrier all around.

"Who are you? What do you want with us?" Xingyin cried, her voice shaking with seeming terror.

The Bone Devil's mouth parted to reveal rows of needle-sharp teeth. A purplish tongue slithered forth to lick its plump lips. "I am hungry, child," it said in a singsong voice. "The cruel Celestials have caged me for too long. I must sate my appetite. You cannot escape, but if you come here and let me feed a little—I will set you and your companion free. It will not hurt."

Lies, I thought bleakly, recalling the bodies left in its wake. Drained of their lifeforce and blood, their expressions locked in horror and agony. I would sacrifice none of my soldiers to this creature's vicious appetite.

"Do you promise to let us go?" I played along with this farce.

"Upon my honor," it swore in honeyed tones as it stalked closer, its gaze darting around to probe our surroundings. Could it sense the wards?

"How can we trust you?" Xingyin asked. A fitting question, for no one would surrender themselves so easily, no matter the assurance.

The Bone Devil took another step closer, its lips curving into a malicious smile, eyes alight with anticipation. It thought it had us snared; we were almost within reach of its arms—even as it neared the boundary of our wards. Xingyin swayed where she stood as though struggling with the impulse, taking a step toward the creature—

It sprang toward us, right through the wards, its eyes widening as it sensed our trap closing around it. I moved swiftly, discarding our illusion, thrusting my sword at its torso. It dipped back, then turned to flee. But it didn't get far, light erupting around us, the wards holding fast.

"Celestial soldiers!" The Bone Devil's shriek pierced my ears. "I will peel your skin from your flesh, rip your limbs from your body," it snarled as it faced us once more.

Rage flashed, which I quenched. It was a vulnerability that an astute enemy would hone into a blade, and the Bone Devil had proven itself a cunning adversary.

Xingyin drew her bow, the tips of three arrows glinting in the light, releasing them to hurtle through the air. The monster crossed its arms, a column of light enveloping it like a cloak. The arrows struck, then fell away, as limp as straw. In the same breath, the Bone Devil dove toward her, its claws slashing at her face.

As she shielded herself, I leapt forward in a reckless assault. My sword arced through the air, cutting the creature relentlessly. Xingyin's magic slammed against its barrier, and when it cracked, her next arrow burst through to plunge into the Bone Devil's arm. Pride flashed through me at how she wielded magic and weapon so seamlessly, one of the first things I'd taught her.

The Bone Devil tore out the arrows, pale liquid oozing from the gashes. As its claws glided over them, the wounds sealed, though its face twisted in unbridled wrath.

"You think you shoot well?" it sneered, flinging its palms wide. Shards of bone erupted from its flesh, hurtling like darts toward Xingyin. She fell to the ground and rolled away, her shield shining brighter. One shard struck, penetrating her barrier, burying into her shoulder. As her blood spilled forth, wrath burned like a hot coal in my gut. Gritting my teeth, I flew at the creature, my sword slamming at it again and again—craving the physical satisfaction of driving my blade through its flesh to sate my rage. The Bone Devil met my blows with equal ferocity, yet it was tiring fast. My magic enveloped it, locking its limbs, as the tip of my blade sank through the creature's chest. It lurched free, then dove at me—its jaws snapping, fangs glistening. I was too close, within its grasp. A careless slip. I moved back but a burst of its power seized me, dragging me forward, its claws poised to sink into my neck. As I braced, a shield sprang up around me—Xingyin's arrows already arcing through the air, slamming into the Bone Devil's shoulder. It cursed, spinning toward her now, its attentions diverted from me.

"Fall back!" I commanded her urgently, not the Celestial Captain eager to clinch victory—my only concern for her safety. I was tempted to summon the other soldiers to aid us, but they were holding the wards as ordered. If they dropped them, the creature would flee.

Xingyin was already fitting another arrow to her bow, never one for obeying orders when her instincts called. As the Bone Devil flew at her, I dove forward to block its path. Her arrows hurtled forth, driving into the monster's skull. A piteous shriek erupted, curved claws groping at the shaft—its hands quivering before falling away, as it collapsed onto the ground. Its eyes fluttered then sank shut, its body twitching in its final throes, that futile struggle to cling to life that I had seen too many times before. Once, I had felt the same remorse that now darkened Xingyin's expression, but it had faded to a shadow . . . one I could almost pretend did not exist.

Around us, the other soldiers emerged from their hiding places. Their faces were drawn and pale from the strain of holding the wards. As they gathered around the Bone Devil, I bent to examine Xingyin's wound, where the shard of bone had struck. Raising my hand, I released my magic into her body. Healing did not come naturally to me; it drained me more than any other enchantment, but this was a small price to pay. It would also deprive the Celestial Prince of the opportunity to approach her when she was weakened. As the color slowly returned to her face, her lips forming a faint smile, a rare satisfaction filled me that had nothing to do with our victory.

"Your own wounds. You should see to them first," she protested.

I ignored the discomfort. "They are just scratches."

"The Bone Devil almost tore out your throat."

"Thank you for stopping it," I told her gravely. She had risked herself for me, putting herself in harm's way without hesitation. I would not forget it.

Her smile widened. "A favor repaid. You've saved me before."

"More than once." Pride spurred the reminder.

"This won't be my last time either." Her gaze held mine. "Friends watch out for each other."

A promise that softened even my hard heart, though it was accompanied by the unwelcome title of friend once again. Yet there was more between us than the friendship she claimed, and her trust was a gift I would not disdain.

A trust I would destroy. I struck the thought away.

Such frail foundations to build a future upon, but I would not waver from the path ahead. Since my youth, I had learned to seize what I wanted, whether through force or cunning. I had been born to a title without its privileges, thrust into a dangerous world, one I had carved my own place in. I would never compromise what I had fought so hard for, that was almost within my grasp. The wiser part of me cautioned against further entanglement, but it was too late. Yet I would be no slave to desire, no fool for love—my heart would never rule my head.

SHUXIAO | 淑晓
RETURN TO THE JADE PALACE

A tale of *Heart of the Sun Warrior*, in which Shuxiao
undertakes a quest to rescue the captive Celestials.

GENERAL MENGQI AND I FLEW in silence upon our cloud, the other soldiers following behind us. They were the "demons" I had feared and dreaded from the tales, but they did not seem markedly different from other immortals. Just more arrogant and unpleasant, I decided, my irritation at the general's earlier condescension unappeased.

"To clear up any doubt, *I* will be in command of this undertaking," General Mengqi announced in a lofty tone, without troubling herself to meet my eye.

I pulled myself up, annoyed that she was taller than me. "You are *not*. I know the Jade Palace, where the hostages are being held. I'll lead the quest." My good sense protested that I was fighting for command out of spite when I typically shied from such things. The burdens of prestige were often not worth their weight. Still, I had volunteered for this task, it was my people that we were rescuing, and I would not wholly entrust their fates to those who'd been our bitterest foes.

"Was your position in the Celestial Army one of worth? Why

were you discharged?" she demanded. "I'll not leave my soldiers in the hands of a stranger, much less an incompetent one."

"You're a poor judge of character if you rely on titles to be a good measure of competence, *General*." I paused, letting my jibe sink in. "It doesn't matter what you think. Wenzhi instructed that I would lead this. Will you disobey his command?"

"Do not refer to His Majesty so casually, you insolent Celestial," she hissed.

"Do not attempt to defy *His Majesty's* command, you witless Demon," I flung back.

I had little respect for their king; I had not forgiven his abduction of my friend, even if his recent attempts to make amends had softened—somewhat—my harsh opinion of him. And not just mine. Xingyin might not realize it, but her struggle to hold on to past grudges was apparent, as was her gradual shift of heart toward the newly crowned king of the Cloud Wall. While it hurt Prince Liwei, whom I bore great respect for, my loyalties were first and foremost to her.

General Mengqi's eyes thinned as she stepped toward me. She moved with a poise and assurance that I would have found attractive in another, except everything about her seemed to rouse my ire. Maybe it was instinct, the wisdom of my inner eye.

"Enough with this childish bickering," she declared, as if she had not started it with her rudeness. "We will lead this together, but do not get in my way." She spoke coldly, enunciating each word as though I could not understand.

"My dear general," I replied with biting sarcasm. "You do not grasp what it means to work together, and you reveal your ignorance with every utterance. We will most definitely get in each other's way unless you adopt a more collaborative attitude."

"How dare you question my attitude?" she snapped. "It is

my soldiers' lives at stake, for I couldn't care less about you Celestials."

"And that's exactly why you should not lead this. Instead of picking these needless fights, you may start by asking if I want to share command rather than ordering me to." I would, of course, discard such trivialities in the face of real danger. But it was a long and uneventful flight to the Celestial Kingdom, and the general had not earned my patience.

Silence fell between us, of the unsettling variety in which I imagined the gnashing of teeth.

"Do you agree to share command?" she ground out at last.

I flashed a wide grin. "Of course."

She nodded curtly. "Now that's settled, what do you know of the Jade Palace? Where do you think the emperor is being held?"

As a Demon, it was unlikely she would have visited the palace before. The change in her attitude was apparent, the rancor gone from her tone. Her ability to put aside personal differences to focus on our task raised my opinion of the general, but only a little.

"The royal family's chambers are at the center of the palace, encircled by the Inner Courtyard, while the soldiers' quarters are closest to the walls. Wugang would want to take the emperor's chamber for himself—a symbol of the power he covets. Yet it's unlikely he would move the emperor out of the area entirely as it's the most secure place. With the Celestial Empress and Crown Prince absent, the hostages would likely be held in one of their courtyards."

She tucked her chin between her fingers, her expression thoughtful. "Why not the prison?"

"They might be there," I conceded. "But I think Wugang would want to keep up appearances, to pretend he has the support of the court. Locking the emperor and the highest ranked courtiers into cells would shatter that illusion, earning the hostility of the Celestial Kingdom's allies. The rest of the Immortal Realm will be looking closely to see how he treats the emperor before determining whether to ally with or move against him. As an experienced courtier, Wugang would know all this."

"You're smarter than you appear," she said grudgingly.

I scowled. "General Mengqi, your compliments sting as badly as your insults."

"Purely intentional."

As a smile formed on her lips, something pulsed inside me. I ignored it, looking away into the distance. "Are we in agreement, that we'll search the royal courtyards first?"

She nodded, dropping her voice though it was just us on the cloud. "But we must be careful. I will take no unnecessary risks; I will not send my soldiers to needless deaths. I do not believe saving your Celestial Emperor—the one who persecuted us all these years—a worthwhile cause."

"Nor do I," I agreed, earning a startled glance from her. "I'm not doing this for His Celestial Majesty, may boils erupt on the soles of his feet."

"Then why?"

"Because Wugang is holding captive some of the best of the Celestial Court, those who tried to stand up to him. General Jianyun, for one."

She paused. "I have heard of this general. Our king served with him when—"

"—he was a spy in the Celestial Army?" I interjected, part of me still furious at the deception, for the high regard I had once held him in.

She stiffened at the slight. "Do not speak of His Majesty so callously. He had little choice, the alternative being to remain powerless and persecuted. He is far worthier of the throne than any other privileged royal, earning it through his own merit. I've served him long enough to know there will be no better ruler."

She spoke with such earnest passion, I could not help wondering if she might harbor feelings for Wenzhi. An unsettling thought as it would be unrequited, for there was only one person in that Demon's icy heart—something that had been clear even in his days as a Celestial Captain. While I did not think him worthy of my friend, neither could I deny the depth of his emotions—and those he seemed to evoke in Xingyin despite her attempts to conceal it.

Still, curiosity pricked me. "What is your relationship with your king?" The question was too personal, bordering on insolent. Yet I wanted to leave nothing to chance, for Wenzhi had fooled us so thoroughly before.

"Are you asking for yourself or your friend?" she said in clipped tones. When I remained silent, she continued, "His Majesty and I have been acquainted since we were children. Threatened by the same scum who could not tolerate one younger yet more accomplished, and a child of lowborn parents as me. I tied my fortunes to him the moment I entered the army, partly from loyalty, and because I knew he would rise higher than those who tried to keep him down."

Her bluntness eased some of the weight pressing upon me. I had felt low since the fight with Wugang on the beach, after being poisoned by his soldier's guandao. My spirits had not been improved by being made to drink an endless stream of foul remedies by the dragons. I had not protested, neither fool nor brave enough to disobey a dragon. Yet my wonder at their presence had been rapidly worn away by dread, whenever one of them appeared with another porcelain bowl.

Somehow, on this cloud, in the general's company tonight, I felt more alive than I had in a long time. General Mengqi was aggravating, yet I was starting to enjoy her company. She did not glaze her words with frivolity, speaking in a frank manner that lent her speech more weight. I wanted to learn more about her, but the Jade Palace loomed on the horizon, its dark green roof agleam in the fading light.

Halting our cloud, I signaled for the other soldiers to do the same. "It will not be easy to gain entrance. The palace is warded against entry, only those with Wugang's permission may enter without incident."

"Shall we create an 'incident'?" General Mengqi asked, running a finger over the hilt of her sword.

I grinned, approving of the direction of her thoughts. "If I recognize someone at the gate, I'll try to convince them to aid us. I know most of the soldiers, though am unsure who remains in Wugang's service. Many who served the previous emperor will not be pleased at this usurpation, though few would dare show it."

"What if you fail? What if they attack you on sight?" She did not appear troubled by the prospect.

"I'll only speak to the ones that won't." Despite the assured way I spoke, my mind darted to the many ways this might go wrong. "If I'm forced to fight, I will need your help," I admitted.

"It depends on the situation," she countered. "I'll not risk my soldiers unnecessarily."

Did she view *my* life alone as dispensable? "If I'm killed, you'll have no hope of getting into the palace," I reminded her tersely.

"Then a few Celestials will die." She shrugged. "There are worse things."

"Yes, that of your esteemed king's anger and disappointment," I retorted.

Her mouth pursed. Wenzhi's opinion mattered to her—as it would with loyalty born of respect, not conferred by obligation.

It said something of his character that Wenzhi was able to earn this from so capable a subordinate, as he had from the Celestials he'd commanded, even those he had no real desire to serve.

"We will keep you safe," she conceded reluctantly. "I'll come with you. I have ways of convincing the stubborn."

Her pupils glinted like onyx as she spoke. I recoiled inwardly, having almost forgotten the fearsome power some of these immortals possessed, the one they had been persecuted for. I did not want her to tamper with another's mind, not if there was another way.

"Let me speak to them first. Wait here, for my signal."

"And if you fail?"

I grimaced. "Then the command will be yours, as you wished."

THE SIGHT OF THE Jade Palace evoked no joy in me, just the gloom of dread. Had it been only weeks since I'd left? It felt like years, a decade . . . for even after all my time here, this place did not feel like home. It never had. There was no warmth in my heart, no rise in my spirits, rather a tight unease at the sight of the walls that ringed the palace.

I flew to the Eastern Gate, keeping a careful distance as I observed the guards there. There were fewer than expected; perhaps most had been mobilized to the Cloud Wall border for the planned assault. Only Wugang's trusted soldiers were on duty here, their pale faces shining, their guandao clasped in their hands. Neither immortal nor mortal, nor of flesh or blood. An involuntary shiver shot down my back as I recalled the accursed blade sliding into my flesh, my body splintering with pain. No, I could not enter through here. There was no hope of convincing these guards, who would obey Wugang's command unquestioningly.

Abandoning the Eastern Gate, I flew to the northern one. It

was smaller, less used because it led to a more circuitous route before reaching the Outer and Inner Courts. Fortunately, this gate was guarded by Celestials in addition to Wugang's troops. The wards woven around it were strong, apparent even at this distance, and I was careful to keep out of reach.

Catching sight of a familiar face, I exhaled with relief, waiting impatiently till he was away from the other soldiers. "Feimao," I whispered, threading a shaft of wind to bear my words to him.

His head swung in my direction. As an archer, his vision was sharp. He turned once as though checking he was alone, before facing toward me again.

"Shuxiao? Why are you here? We were ordered to apprehend you on sight."

It was a relief that he did not call for reinforcements right away. "Will you?" I asked to be sure, for he would not lie to my face.

He shook his head. "We've lost too many of us already."

His choice of words gladdened me, that he regarded me as one of them. "Why aren't you at the border with the Celestial Army?"

"Celestial Army?" Feimao repeated scathingly. "It no longer deserves the name. We know what Wugang's new recruits are, no matter what he claims. We recognize those spirits—our fallen friends and comrades harnessed into this . . . vile slavery. Such wickedness. What will happen to the rest of us? We only survived this long because we hid our anger, feigning obedience—but Wugang trusts none of us, except his own soldiers."

For good reason, I thought. "You know where my loyalties lie, and they're not with the false emperor." I restrained myself from plunging onward to ask his aid. Persuasion was a delicate skill, more powerful when one did not realize they were being guided. A vital part of it lay in the ability to listen, to discern the clues to form a connection. I didn't want to manipulate Feimao, but I did need to convince him.

"Wugang is false indeed," Feimao agreed bitterly. "He was not much of a general before, quick to punish, only rewarding those wholly loyal to him. He's no better as an emperor, seeing threats everywhere and in everyone, except those who have no will but his."

"What future is there in serving such a leader?" I prodded, glad for the opening he had provided. "His entire ambition is founded upon avenging the insult to his pride, bearing a grudge even though the perpetrators are dead by his own hand. Wugang does not care for the realm; he will lead us into ruin." I spoke slowly, letting my words sink in. "Do you not have reservations? Is that why you're not fighting the battle?"

His lips thinned. "I did not want to fight. I do not believe in the cause."

"They allowed you to refuse?"

"My archery skills have deteriorated markedly of late. An injury to the arm." I heard the wink in his words. "I have no interest in playing Wugang's games. I wanted to remain here to keep an eye on those I care for."

"General Jianyun? He is why I'm here," I told him.

He nodded briefly. "What of His Celestial Majesty? How do you intend to get them out?"

I had no love for the emperor, but for now, our interests were aligned. "Help me get into the palace. I will rescue him."

He frowned. "Shuxiao, we can't do this alone. While the guard is reduced of late, there are still too many soldiers around. Some watch the gates, but others are in the empress's courtyard where the hostages are held."

"We won't be alone. I've brought reinforcements."

"Who?"

"Soldiers from the Cloud Wall." I'd considered not telling him but it would be a betrayal of his trust, which might hurt us more in the end.

He drew back in apparent outrage. "You're working with the *Demons*?"

"I'm working with *allies*. We need all the help we can get. Sometimes it takes a greater monster to put everything into perspective," I said with feeling. "Prince Liwei sent me to secure the hostages. They are in grave danger because of the impending battle. If we do not save them, they could be killed. I have His Highness's trust, as do those who fight with me. Will you help us?"

As Feimao hesitated, I held my breath. "If that is His Highness's wish, I will obey," he said at last. "I'll pretend I hear a disturbance beyond the walls. Some of the guards will leave with me to investigate, a few will remain. Do not attempt to enter then—wait till I return, conceal yourself and your aura. We will enter the palace together and with luck, they'll miss your presence in the upheaval." He added, "I'd never have attempted this under General Jianyun's watch, but Wugang is not the leader he imagines he is. Moreover, while his soldiers are obedient, they do not respond effectively to unforeseen circumstances when he's not around to guide them."

"What if they discover us?" I asked.

"Then I hope your reinforcements are close, and that the Demons fight as well as they are reputed to," he replied solemnly.

As I nodded, Feimao cried out to the other guards, gesturing in the opposite direction from where I hid. "Someone just flew past! An intruder!"

The soldiers gathered soundlessly, giving no other sign of acknowledgment. Clouds descended, hovering beside them. As Feimao mounted one, a soldier moved to climb up behind him, but Feimao blocked his path. "I will go ahead to catch them. We are faster when flying alone."

As they ascended to the skies, the wind churned violently around me. The sun was now a scarlet disc, its rays burnishing the dragons on the roof, the jade tiles shining as though wet with rain. Recalling General Mengqi and her soldiers, I channeled a flare of light as a signal. Shortly after, the general appeared, flying toward me.

"You were gone a long time," she remarked. "What happened?"

"An old friend will help me enter," I said without preamble.

"What about the rest of us?"

"Remain here, close by the gate. Once I free the hostages, we'll need your aid to escape."

She frowned. "I'll come with you. My second-in-command can take charge of those remaining here. They will wait for our return."

If we make it that far. I buried the thought. "Why do you want to come?"

"I'm not one for sitting on the sidelines." She cocked her head to one side. "I'm also curious about the Jade Palace. It's a rare opportunity to scope out enemy terrain."

A habitual protest rose, but I ignored it. After the battle, the kingdoms would either be bound closer in alliance . . . or crushed beneath Wugang's yoke. A sobering reminder of all that was at stake. Without waiting for my response, General Mengqi left to speak to her soldiers. When she returned, we wove a shield to cloak our forms.

We did not have long to wait. Feimao soon emerged, flying toward us. "Is this the Demon?" He peered suspiciously at General Mengqi as though expecting her to sprout another head.

"*Demon* is not quite the insult you Celestials imagine it is,"

General Mengqi hissed. "It lends an air of terror that can be useful when facing cowards."

I was tempted to laugh at Feimao's furious expression, but we needed his help. "Don't mind her; she has a tendency to offend everyone. Can you bring us both over the wall?"

Feimao gestured for us to ascend his cloud. "The moment we land, make your way as quickly as you can. I can't leave without arousing suspicion, but once you've rescued the hostages, head to the Northern Gate. I'll fight by your side then, if need be."

"Thank you," I told him gratefully.

He inclined his head. "Thank you for doing what we cannot. May His Celestial Majesty and General Jianyun be safe."

"May they all be," I murmured.

We plunged through the wards. Before the cloud had even halted, I leapt from it, running away from the gate. General Mengqi's footsteps padded close behind as we made our way carefully to a deserted courtyard, the one Xingyin and Prince Liwei had used to slip from the Jade Palace. Most of the older guards were aware of their subterfuge though we'd said nothing, allowing them this illusion.

"The hostages are in the empress's courtyard," I told the general in hushed tones. "We must secure their safety first. Once released, they can fight with us."

"If they are able to," General Mengqi said grimly.

A chilling thought; it hadn't occurred to me that they might be incapacitated. What if they had been injured? Tortured? I reined in my worries. If they were hurt, all the more reason to make haste. As we headed to the Celestial Empress's courtyard, it struck me that I'd never been there before. A relief, for the empress only ever summoned someone to reprimand or punish them.

Long-tailed phoenixes were carved on the entrance, their gilded beaks and wings studded with gems. A pair of flowering trees flanked the doors, their blossoms a vibrant scarlet with yellow centers.

"Eight soldiers." General Mengqi examined the guards. "Though there are undoubtedly more within."

"One is more than enough," I warned her. "Don't underestimate them. Wugang's soldiers feel no pain nor fear, and while fire can harm them, they regenerate so quickly any injury is short-lived. Nor can you enchant their minds—Wenzhi tried. Worse yet, their guandao leeches our lifeforce. I've seen them slay an immortal with a single blow." My chest constricted at the recollection.

"Is that all?" she asked brusquely, maybe to veil her own unease. "No iron talons, venomous claws, or breath of flame?"

I fought back an unexpected smile. "They are obedient but lack independence. If we hold the element of surprise, we stand a chance. But we must keep the turmoil contained to the empress's courtyard." I added, "I will keep them occupied while you free the hostages. Conceal yourself, and do not engage with the guards."

I was not keen to dive headlong into danger as bait, but she was not a Celestial; this was not her fight. Moreover, I had faced Wugang's soldiers before and . . . I did not want her hurt.

She studied my face. "A fair plan. Except I should distract the guards while you save the others."

I shook my head. "No—"

She continued, speaking over my protest. "The emperor will never agree to leave with me, a Demon. We must liberate the hostages as quickly as possible, to escape. You are best equipped for that."

It was true, yet guilt surged to have her undertake the more perilous task. Just a single cut from those guandao—I suppressed the thought. "You must stay out of reach of their weapons. You can't let them capture you."

"I won't. I'll try to keep them in the courtyard, but you'll need to silence the sounds within. There will be enough to deal with without any reinforcements." She smiled tightly. "Don't take too long."

"I won't," I assured her.

I released my energy, crafting a spell of privacy, stretching it painstakingly across the breadth of the courtyard. It was sparsely woven, easily snapped—but it would have to suffice.

General Mengqi drew her sword, her blade reflecting the pale light. Night was almost upon us, a disadvantage, for we could not see as well in the dark. As she raised her hand, fire flashed from her palms—gliding across the doors, devouring the wood like paper. As the guards rushed toward her, she ducked below the blazing doorway and raced out of their reach.

My heart was thudding so hard, I thought it might burst. Was I afraid for myself or her? Likely both, as our survival was entwined. There was no time to waste. No matter the general's skill, she could not hold off those creatures for long. Swiftly, I scaled the walls, dropping to the other side. There were more guards within, already heading in the direction of General Mengqi's commotion. I allowed myself one backward glance to find her running through the courtyard. Fortunately, the vast grounds provided ample space to lose oneself among the bamboo groves, flower bushes, and secluded pavilions.

I slunk along the walls, keeping to the shadows, straining to keep the privacy spell intact. If it broke, the ruckus would draw every guard in the palace to us. The doors to the empress's chamber were locked but unguarded—perhaps the soldiers had been led away. I swept my hand over the doors, channeling my energy. The wooden panels broke apart, swinging open. Darkness yawned within, the curtains drawn, but I darted inside without hesitation. Pulling the doors shut behind me, I spun around, my shadow thrown long by the flickering light of a single lantern.

My blood went cold. The eerie sight before me seemed plucked from a nightmare. The Celestial Emperor was seated at the end of the room, upon a red-lacquered chair, carved into a pattern of phoenix wings. General Jianyun, Teacher Daoming, and several other high-ranking courtiers were arranged around him. Their arms lay on the wooden armrests, their backs pulled straight. They were as still as statues, a waxy sheen glazing their ashen skin, their eyes wide and unfocused like they could not see. Were they . . . dead? No, if Wugang had killed them, there would be no need to guard this place. How long had they sat in this position? Were they asleep, or enchanted to remain awake in this frozen state—a torment to the body and mind? If this was vengeance, it was of the most malevolent kind.

I rushed to General Jianyun first. His gaze remained blank, yielding no sign he was aware of my presence. As I touched his hand, pain blistered my fingers, erupting across my arm. I formed a shield at once, halting the strange magic and wrenching my hand free. My breathing was labored, sweat breaking out over my forehead. General Jianyun twitched then, his eyes blinking rapidly. I dared not touch him again, gathering my power and releasing it into his body. A strange energy seemed to suffuse him from within, pinning him into place. Carefully, I plucked apart these magical binds, like thorns embedded in his flesh. With each one gone, the spell weakened—until at last, General Jianyun sucked in a drawn breath and slumped forward. I grasped his shoulders to steady him, flinching from the ice of his skin, relief surging as the waxiness of his pallor faded.

"His Celestial Majesty. The others—" he gasped hoarsely.

As he staggered to his feet, making his way to the emperor, I hurried to Teacher Daoming. Swiftly, I worked to free her from the enchantment, just as General Jianyun's energy streaked over the emperor. His Celestial Majesty stirred, blinking furtively as he fell back against the chair, his body curled inward. General Jianyun, Teacher Daoming, and I rushed to free the rest of the courtiers. They were shaken from the ordeal, and utterly furious.

"Wugang must be punished," a minister snarled. "How dare he do such a thing? Imprisoning us. Proclaiming himself emperor. Our troops and allies will never stand for this."

"He will pay." The Celestial Emperor spoke now, though his tone was hollow, his hands trembling.

"We must get out of the palace first." Once, I might have quailed before such a distinguished audience, but urgency dimmed such concerns. I hurried to the entrance, thinking of General Mengqi in danger, outside. "Be on your guard. The soldiers—"

"Where is my army?" the emperor demanded. "Surely, they have come to my rescue. Surely, they would not serve that *traitor*."

I turned to him. "Your Celestial Majesty, your army is no more. Wugang's undead have filled the ranks. Those who remained did what they needed to survive, to assist from within." My words were calculated to ensure no anger fell upon Feimao and the others. "It is the Cloud Wall who helped with this rescue."

"Cloud Wall?" the emperor sputtered, his face going red then white.

How I wished Xingyin could have seen him in this state. Their Celestial Majesties had been unkind to her, humiliating and suspecting her at every turn. They had been wrong; she was not their enemy. They had been blinded by flattery and an overblown sense of their own superiority, tripped over by ill judgment. If Wugang's treachery had not spread across the realm like a vile contagion, I would have been content to see Their Celestial Majesties remain humbled.

"Yes, the Cloud Wall." I enunciated the words. "One of their generals is outside as we speak, risking herself to keep Wugang's soldiers at bay. We have no time to lose. We must help her, before we escape."

Without another word, I stalked outside, the others following me. The courtyard was plunged into chaos, plants and flowers trampled, flames eating into the columns of a pavilion. General Mengqi was surrounded by Wugang's soldiers, fire flashing from her blade as she swept it in a wide arc, the soldiers skittering around her.

Clouds swooped from the skies, descending by the emperor's feet. As he stepped upon one, followed by the other courtiers, I seethed. How could they flee before ensuring *all* of us were safe? We had risked ourselves to save them, while they cared not for our lives. Selfish cowards, the lot of them. But I would not abandon my allies. I plunged forward, hacking at one of the soldiers, eager to carve a path for General Mengqi to break free.

I was grateful to find General Jianyun fighting beside me, as was Teacher Daoming—our attacks creating a narrow opening.

"Hurry!" I called to General Mengqi, summoning a cloud at the same time. She raced toward us, ducking between the guards' blows. We leapt upon the cloud, soaring into the skies, as high as the wards of the palace permitted. My nerves were frayed as we neared the Northern Gate, enemy clouds rising in pursuit as Wugang's soldiers took flight—though the Celestial Emperor and his courtiers were far ahead of us.

"A barrier has been erected around the walls," General Jianyun warned.

The air stirred as he and Teacher Daoming gathered their energy and flung it out in a glowing wave. It streaked across an unseen shield, shuddering, though it remained intact. In the distance, the Celestial Emperor raised his hands, a torrent of power surging forth in streaks of white and gold, forming a blizzard that slammed against the shield, piercing its surface. It shattered then, fragments scattering like hail.

Unhindered, we shot over the walls—Wugang's soldiers firmly on our trail. Magic flowed from our hands to spur our flight, yet they gained on us with each moment. Just ahead, the Cloud Wall soldiers appeared from where they were hiding. A fog closed around them, stretching to obscure us from sight. They flew among us in a winding pattern, splintering across the sky to throw off our pursuers and draw them away. General Mengqi had trained them well.

I breathed easier then, my relief spreading as I glanced back to find Feimao mounting a cloud of his own, flying away from the Jade Palace. It was no longer safe for him to remain, particularly if Wugang emerged victorious today.

Someone came to stand beside me. "Thank you," General Mengqi said, clasping her hands behind her back. "For a moment, I thought I'd be left behind."

I stared at her in disbelief. "Then you do not owe me thanks, but an apology. Is your opinion of me so low?"

"It's not high for all Celestials," she admitted. "Though it has improved of late."

I grinned, relishing this newfound ease between us. "I hope it will continue to improve."

Her head bent in my direction, her gaze appraising—but not in the way that had offended me earlier. It seemed more intimate, less calculating. Or maybe I now saw her in a different light.

"It depends on the company I keep."

"I feel the same way about Demons," I told her.

"Then . . . shall we endeavor to change each other's minds?" she asked a trace tentatively.

Was that an invitation? Did a flush color her cheeks? As she smiled at me, my heart lifted, and I found myself inclined to accept her invitation . . . because I wanted to see her again.

LIWEI | 力伟
A RIVAL'S SPIRIT

A tale of *Heart of the Sun Warrior*, after the final battle,
once Liwei has ascended the throne.

———

THE MOON WAS A BRIGHT curve, ringed by stars. Will there ever come a time that I look upon them and not think of her? I longed for and dreaded the day. I moved away from the window, sitting by my desk. Leaning against the chair, I closed my eyes. In the dark, I could almost imagine the lilting strains of Xingyin's flute, just as when she had played for me in my courtyard, before the cares of the kingdom had consumed us. Just this echo of a memory was enough to warm my heart, to stir cold regret.

I had wanted her to be part of my life here, believing there was nothing more important than being the Celestial Emperor. While I had never craved the power of the throne, neither would I discard my duty. If she could have been content here, my happiness would have been complete. But while this was my home, it had never been hers. The years we spent together were precious ones, and I wished we'd had more time to live freely as we'd dreamed of—but life had taken an abrupt turn, hurting us both.

We had tried to repair that which was broken, almost suc-
ceeding in building something new—yet it was never as strong
as before, like trying to smooth a folded web. Had that been my
mistake, hoping she would fit into my life, rather than wanting
what was best for her? Should I have guided her better in her
dealings with the Celestial Court, in how to win my parents'
favor? Her life would have been easier, yet it would have turned
her into someone she was not. I should not have expected her
to change for me, but in the darkest of times when I longed for
her . . .

How I wished she could have.

A selfish thought. Xingyin had given so much of herself, beginning with her love that I'd first cast aside. Even after, she had
stood by me, defended and protected me, rescuing our realm

from Wugang's villainy. I'd thought nothing could break her, but I was wrong. No one was invulnerable. Those stronger might endure more, but they paid for it, nonetheless.

She did not think she was a hero, but she was mine. She gave of herself without resentment or calculation, even as it drained her. In the worst days of her own grief, she had stayed here, trying to ease my burdens. Having just lost my mother and gained a throne—one weakened by Wugang's treachery—I had leaned on her, accepting her comfort with little thought for hers. At first, I'd not understood the depths of her grief, and later—I had been unwilling to speak of it, to acknowledge how much *he* meant to her, and what that meant for us. I'd believed as long as we were together, I could make things right, that she would forget. It might have been true once, but no more. When she had left the Jade Palace, her spirit was almost broken . . . and I had let her go.

Xingyin thought her heart divided, and mine was, too—though in a different way. I loved my kingdom and my people. They gave my life purpose, direction, and warmth, long before I had met the moon goddess's daughter. Just as she had always done what she thought was right, so had I. Just as she would not have been happy here, neither would I have been roaming the realm, knowing I had abandoned my kingdom when it most needed me. Guilt would have eaten at me until it leeched all contentment. There was peace in my choice now, no matter what it had cost me.

A tightness formed in my chest. This night seemed one for unearthing bitter truths, unwanted though they were. I should not envy the dead, but Xingyin possessed a connection with the Demon—different from ours, yet no less profound. She felt more for him than she had admitted, or only realized it too late. As for him, he had learned his lesson better than I had, pursuing her with unwavering dedication, risking everything, even choosing her life over his.

Resting my elbows on the desk, I wrenched my mind back to the work that awaited. Caring for the realms was an endless task. There was immense satisfaction in resolving the matters of the kingdom, in extending a hand to those in need, to right the wrongs and injustices that plagued the people. Their gratitude and adulation offered a joy I had not known before, a quieter one that I grew to appreciate.

I missed Xingyin still, but she was not lost to me. Our bond was rooted in friendship, remaining even after all else had withered. She would come if I needed her, though she might not stay. And if there was ever anything I could do for her, she had but to ask.

I would not pity myself. I was the Emperor of the Celestial Kingdom, ruling over the skies and earth. Nor did I intend to live alone forever, lost in the past. I would choose a partner who would grace my world and cherish it. One I might grow to love. While it might not be the love I had imagined, it need not be any less. Life was not perfect; there were always hidden wounds, pain disguised beneath a smile, a price to any happiness possessed. We had to bear our burdens the best we could, for we alone knew their true weight.

I picked up a scroll and unrolled the thick brocade. A message from the Eastern Sea requesting an exchange of military commanders. It would be a favor on our part, for our soldiers were better trained and more experienced, but it would benefit us to strengthen our loyal allies in the Four Seas. I wrote a favorable reply to their king, then reached for another scroll—an urgent missive from the Golden Desert, from their new ruler who had united the tribes. From what we'd heard, not all welcomed this change—some protested, but it seemed under control.

My fingers tapped the table in a restless rhythm as I read. The Winged Devils were gathering in the Golden Desert. While their numbers were small, a trickle could swell into a flood, if untended. These creatures had not openly defied us before, but they were loosely allied with others more powerful and infinitely more dangerous. New problems cropped up quicker than I could settle them. Was this how my father had let things slide? Not from indifference, but because there was far too much for one— even an immortal—to bear?

I set the scroll aside, deciding to seek General Jianyun's advice. Part of me wanted to send the Celestial Army to stop them at once, but we had to learn why they were here. They had made little effort to conceal their presence, yet done nothing to warrant our interference. If this was a diversion, moving too quickly would be playing into their hands, leaving the greater plan uncovered. Governance was a fine balance, the urge to act tempered by the reality of consequence.

As I reached for another scroll, someone knocked on the door. An attendant stood in the entrance, her eyes cast down as she bowed. "Your Celestial Majesty, the Keeper of Mortal Fates and General Jianyun request an audience."

I gestured for them to enter, even as a knot formed in my gut. They would not be here at this hour unless it was a matter of grave importance. As they bowed before me, I wasted no time in asking, "Honored Keeper, is the Mortal Realm at peace?"

"Your Celestial Majesty, we are here to report on an unusual phenomenon." He cleared his throat, adding, "By the Cloud Wall."

My hands clenched before I could stop them. I forced my fingers to straighten, placing them upon my lap. "What is happening there?"

"A surge of power along the border of the Golden Desert," General Jianyun elaborated. "We think it's him. The Cloud Wall King."

"He is dead," I said flatly, hardening myself. I would have no pity for him. Traitor to my people, a liar and deceiver. The one who had taken Xingyin from me.

"His spirit still lingers there. We detected traces before, and observed it as previously instructed by Your Celestial Majesty," the Keeper continued, undaunted. "Back then, even though the laurel had preserved part of his consciousness, it was not enough to restore him."

"However, his spirit seems to be growing stronger," General Jianyun said.

"How is that possible?" I asked brusquely. "Is it the laurel? Was it not destroyed?"

"The laurel was incinerated to ash," General Jianyun replied. "Something else is keeping his spirit here, strengthening it, even. We aren't sure what or how."

"Or who," the Keeper of Mortal Fates added quietly.

A faint suspicion bloomed in my mind. Xingyin—who else would have such a hold over him, reaching beyond death itself?

"What was not possible before, may be now," General Jianyun said delicately. "We might be able to send him to the Mortal Realm in preparation for his eventual return—"

"But only if Your Celestial Majesty wishes it," the Keeper interjected as he stroked his beard.

No, I did not *wish* it; I was not made of stone. Back then, my heart had been softened by Xingyin's suffering and his sacrifice. I had wanted to do anything in my power to ease her grief, even aiding the one I loathed and resented above all. I still wanted to help her, and yet . . . over the years, I had grown accustomed to putting him from my mind, to a world without his existence. Selfishness had set in. Why did he deserve a second chance? Why should he have what I could not?

The unwelcome weight of this decision settled over me. Yet neither the Golden Desert nor Cloud Wall fell within my domain. There was neither need nor reason to venture there, to torment myself further. Glancing down, I found the scroll crumpled between my hands. I smoothed it out, rebuking myself for the lapse in control.

"General Jianyun, Honored Keeper—it is late. Let us speak no more on the matter." My tone allowed no dissent.

They exchanged a long look before leaving the room. More than high-ranking courtiers, they had been my respected teachers—and now, were my most trusted advisors. They had taught Xingyin, too, and watched over her well-being as they did mine. But I had issued an official command. I had not invited their opinion; I did not want to hear it.

I rose and left the room. An attendant followed me, holding a lantern to light the way ahead—the same one who had ushered in my visitors. By the door to my inner chamber, she halted and turned. Her cheeks were flushed, her fingers tightening over the lantern's handle as she took a step toward me. She was lovely, with doe-like eyes and delicate features, her long hair reaching down to her waist. Maybe my defenses were low after tonight's recollections, but an unexpected heat stirred within. It had been a long time since I had felt this whisper of desire. A temptation to lose myself in another's warmth, to feel their arms around me, to indulge in their gentle caresses. Was that not preferable to a solitary bed?

As I stood there, unspeaking, her eyes gleamed. At once, she lowered them, biting her red lip. "May I attend to you tonight, Your Celestial Majesty?" she murmured, her voice dipping low.

The brief spell broke. Memories of Xingyin rushed over me. There had been no artifice about her, no false modesty. I did not want another, at least not tonight.

I shook my head, my tone clipped. "You may leave."

A frown wrinkled her brow, swiftly concealed beneath a smile, as she bowed and backed away. Her emotions seemed a mask to be worn or discarded at will, and I was attuned to disingenuity. She was likely trained to be such a pawn, to be thrust into any situation where she might gain advantage for her mistress. Or perhaps she was merely ambitious, seeking to trade her favors the best way she could. My father might have accepted these offerings with callous ease—but such manipulation left me cold, desire the last thing on my mind.

I could not sleep that night, plagued by restless tension. It did not feel right, ignoring what General Jianyun and the Keeper of Mortal Fates had told me. No matter how much I'd despised the Demon in life, I owed him a debt for the honor of his sacrifice. Few called them by this name now, but it was easier to hate him as a Demon. Still, he had kept Xingyin alive, shielding her from the full extent of Wugang's wrath until we were close enough to aid her. He had died protecting her, and in doing so, protected our realm.

Was that why she could not forget him? I would not delude myself that she loved him *because* of that, she had loved him even before. The memory of their kiss in the Fragrant Mulberry Grove still haunted me, the way their bodies had fit together, how she had gazed at him—just as she used to look at me. I had lost her long before the Demon breathed his last.

Rising from the bed, I shrugged on a robe and pulled my hair into a topknot. As I left the room, the guards followed close behind. They were used to me waking at odd hours of the day, but I did not head to my study as expected, instead making my way toward the main gate of the Jade Palace.

One of the soldiers cleared her throat. "Your Celestial Majesty, if you wish to leave the palace, shall we inform General Jianyun?"

"He is not my nursemaid." I spoke sternly, my temper strained. Yet she was right to caution me, particularly given the recent unrest in the Golden Desert, and our tenuous relationship with the Cloud Wall. I could no longer be reckless, for I *was* the crown. Any harm to me would be inflicted upon the honor of the Celestial Kingdom.

"Summon a troop of guards to accompany us," I said more evenly.

The moment they arrived, we took to our clouds. I flew alone, the soldiers closing behind me. The wind was cold, the sky black. Amid the wildness of flight, I inhaled deeply, relishing the freedom of unfettered horizons. It had been too long since I had left the palace, its willing prisoner. I should walk among my people, hear their words rather than read them in petitions. To live a life of flesh and blood, rather than that of a statue upon a pedestal.

The sands of the desert gleamed almost white in the moonlight. As our clouds descended, I addressed the soldiers. "Wait here. I will go on alone."

"Your Celestial Majesty, it could be dangerous," one of them said anxiously. "Would you allow some of us to accompany you?"

"Do you doubt I can defend myself?" It annoyed me that they thought me helpless when I had trained alongside them for years. "I will shield myself. There is nothing here but sand and cloud."

The guards exchanged wary glances, but they dared not raise another objection. It wasn't merely the solitude I craved tonight, though I did want to be alone. This place evoked too many searing recollections, those that struck too deep to conceal. Moreover, if there was really another presence here, I wanted no witness to our encounter.

As I walked onward, doubts assailed me. Why had I come here? Was it curiosity? The desire for closure? A part of me wanted to confront him—if he were alive, I would have taken satisfaction in striking him as he deserved. Except such sentiments belonged to the past—stray fragments, echoes, shadows of who we had been.

By the edge of the border, I stopped. While relations had improved beneath the reign of their queen, our previous treaty still held; we could not cross into the Cloud Wall without permission. It had not mattered, for few Celestials wanted to venture here, most clinging to old beliefs and prejudices. I would not break this tentative peace; they would have no reason to move against us. Despite our brief alliance against Wugang, I did not trust them. Too much resentment still lay on both sides, particularly after the death of their king.

Carefully, I examined the energy that surrounded this place. An unfamiliar fragrance was entwined with the air, a trace of pine. Drawing a slow breath, I reached out with my magic, seeking that which remained unseen. My Talent in Life yielded a keen awareness of an immortal's presence, even the shade of one. I sifted through the stillness patiently—until I sensed him. His spirit, whatever remained of it.

"Why are you here?" I felt foolish speaking aloud, for attempting to converse with a spirit. They could not talk, they could not feel, they were lost to us. Yet why did I sense the tension I had always felt around him? The awareness of his presence, though it defied all we knew.

There was no reply. Relief flashed as I turned away, but then a wave of cold coursed over me, water droplets beading on the backs of my hands, spreading up my arms. Yet the skies were clear of cloud or rain. A spirit could not control the elements . . .

however the Demon had been no ordinary immortal, but one of the most powerful of our realm.

I waited. To appear in any form would be a great exertion on his part. Something shimmered before me, a clustering of lights, so pale they seemed a trail of dusk.

"What do you want?" I asked aloud.

The lights shivered, a whisper sliding into my consciousness: *The Mortal Realm. Will you send me there?* The words came disjointed, as though it was a great effort to speak. But it was undoubtedly him.

"Why?" I was in no mood to be gracious. He brought out the worst in me, even when he was dead.

A long silence ensued before his next words drifted forth. *I sensed nothing at first, when she came. But she returned again and again, weeping as she spoke to me, until one day . . . I woke from oblivion. She needs me. As I need her.*

It hurt to hear this. He did not mean to be cruel or to gloat; he was a shadow of a spirit, clinging to a scrap of remembrance— yet it stung all the same. Channeling my magic, I crafted an enchantment to strengthen the bond through which he spoke, making it easier for his words to form.

"You do not deserve her," I told him fiercely.

I will endeavor to.

"Why have you not spoken to Xingyin yourself?" I demanded.

She grieves still. I do not want to raise her hopes without reason. I will not cause her more pain.

My chest constricted. I thought he would selfishly bind her to him, even in death. Yet he wanted what was best for her—as should I.

If you will not do this, I will not blame you. Before, if I could have won her from you, I would have spared you no concern. As the voice paused, I fought back a wave of anger.

But if you refuse, then end what is left here, so she will stop coming. I do not want to bind her to futile hope. I want her to live.

"Even with me?" It was not a taunt but a test.

Yes, even with you. The words shot out furiously, before gentling to add, *If that is her choice.*

Confusion warred within, old desires I'd thought laid to rest resurfacing with a vengeance—for what I *should* do and what I *wanted* to were wholly different things. Back then, it had not been possible to restore Wenzhi, there was no true decision to be made. Now I was faced with it, and the prospect of closing forever a door I wanted to keep open. These past years when we believed him gone, I'd let my mind wander on occasion, imagining that Xingyin might one day return to me after she'd made her peace with her loss. But even if it were possible . . . I did not want her that way, to be someone she settled for. A consolation prize. Once, I'd believed it would be enough; I would have said almost anything then to keep her with me. But we both deserved better.

I would not be selfish, not with her. Xingyin should have this chance with the one she had chosen. As for him, a grudging respect solidified at his resolve, at what he would do to return—battling from death itself, to find his way back to her. After everything, Xingyin would have someone who would place her first, keep her safe, cherish her happiness above all— even his own.

How I wanted that kind of love, that all-consuming passion she had given me once. I would find it again. I would do this for her and for me, for all we had been to each other.

"I will help you." I ignored the wrench in my heart. "I will allow you to enter the Mortal Realm and live among them, until you are able to return to our world. As a mortal you will remember none of this, yet your immortal memories and power will be preserved, to be restored upon your return to our realm."

What is the price, Your Celestial Majesty? I never imagined you would agree so easily, without even the pleasure of making me grovel.

"There is nothing easy about this," I said honestly. "I loathe you still. But I trust you love her, as she loves you. Just know this: if you ever hurt her, I will destroy your body and spirit, burying it in the Four Seas."

The lights flared brighter. *You are welcome to try.* A harshness edged the spirit's words, arrogant even in death. *But you will never have cause.*

His answer should have stoked my anger, yet his unflinching pledge granted peace. From my waist, I plucked a yellow jade ornament, one that had been mined from the Mortal Realm. It would hold the essence of his spirit, allowing it to be claimed by a mortal form.

"Gather your spirit."

Thank you, Your Celestial Majesty. He spoke so gravely, with such sincerity, my eyes were damp.

The air shuddered violently, sand springing high. The glittering specks of Wenzhi's spirit arched around the stone, then coalesced into a single luminous sphere. It drifted in the air, sinking into the jade like ink onto silk. The stone gleamed, turning cold to my touch, a sheen of frost coating it now. I wrapped it with a piece of cloth and tucked it securely into my sash.

Tomorrow, I would hand these fragments of his spirit to the Keeper of Mortal Fates. Wenzhi would descend to the realm below, leaving our world. Gradually, the echoes of his presence would fade from here—until not a trace remained. I did not know how long that would take, but I braced, knowing Xingyin would come to me then. While she had kept her distance all this time, once she sensed the absence of Wenzhi's spirit, she would come in search of answers . . . and I would give them to her. An ache twisted within, a soundless protest—but it was tempered by a newfound warmth, sweeping away the lingering remnants of jealousy and of loss.

It would be a joy to banish her misery, to return hope to her life. And perhaps once she was at peace, I would then find mine.

DAWN

WENZHI | 文智
SUN MOON TEAHOUSE

After the end of *Heart of the Sun Warrior*, when Xingyin
meets Wenzhi again in the Mortal Realm.

———

THE LIGHT OF THE EVENING sun slanted through the window, casting the room in gold. Sunset was approaching, the moment I had been anticipating since yesterday. My attendant tentatively offered me a black brocade sash, unused to my indecision. I was not myself, having discarded his previous suggestions. But now, impatient to be on my way, I tied the sash around my waist, then straightened the folds of my robe. My sister would laugh if she knew how I'd deliberated over my attire tonight, wanting to impress my guest, yet not flaunt my wealth. I sensed the young woman I was meeting would care little for it. Never had I troubled myself over what another thought of me, until now. As I told her yesterday, I felt we had met before—and while she assured me that we had, I could not fathom ever forgetting her.

It was not her appearance that caught my attention, though she was certainly striking. Was it her assured manner? Her natural grace, devoid of deliberation? Or the wisdom beyond her years reflected in her eyes? Even now, my mind brimmed with recollections of our brief encounter, my heart quickening in anticipation of the evening ahead. No one had ever elicited such a response from me before. While there had been others—beautiful, noble-born, accomplished—something about the woman from yesterday filled me with wonder.

As first, I had tried to dismiss this inexplicable connection, to reason it away. Yet she must have felt something, too, as she remained to speak to me, in no hurry to leave. Moreover, her acceptance of my invitation meant she wished to see me again.

Unfamiliar emotions gripped me, those I had disdained before from the books and plays. Heat stirred my blood as I recalled the way she moved, the curve of her lips, the arch of her neck. Was this desire? I wanted her as I'd never wanted another, but I would not belittle what I felt. More than physical attraction, I had been unwilling to leave her side—not until I'd elicited a promise from her to meet again. I would have asked to see her that same day, if I had not feared she would balk at my presumption.

I left my home, striding briskly through the streets, eager to reach the teahouse though it was still early. As I entered, the proprietor hurried to greet me, bowing low.

"Honored Minister, do you wish your usual table in the court-yard, the one overlooking the lake?"

"Yes, with one exception," I told her. "Tonight, I would like the sole use of your garden."

Her gaze brightened with avarice. She would agree, I just had to secure the price. "The weather is fine today," she sighed in seeming regret, already calculating what she might extract in compensation. "Many customers will be disappointed for the best view of the lake is from the courtyard."

"I trust you can make them comfortable elsewhere?" I handed her a pouch, the silver within more than a month's rent.

"Honored Minister is far too generous. I dare not accept."

Despite her meek words, her fingers deftly untied the cords of the pouch. As she peeked inside, her eyes rounded.

"It is only fair," I said with a smile. "I would also like screens erected around the pavilion so none of the other guests may see us. And you must serve your finest wine and food."

"We would never dare serve you anything but our best," she protested swiftly. "Would you like a musician and singer to accompany your meal?"

Music was a passion of mine, yet tonight I did not want the intrusion of strangers. "Could you arrange for a qin to be left in the pavilion? I might play myself."

"Honored Minister, this must be a special guest indeed." Curiosity pulsed in her tone, edged with speculation.

"She is," I said gravely. "Be sure to treat her with respect."

"We will, Honored Minister. How many attendants do you wish to serve you and your guest this evening?"

"None." I spoke adamantly to stave off objection. "They may leave after bringing the meal."

The attendants would be certain to report anything we said, for the teahouse owner was as famed for her gossip as she was for her wines. A warning hovered on my tongue, to caution her against spreading rumors, but that would be akin to setting tinder afire. Furthermore, the circulation of such news might offer a welcome respite from the matchmakers who ruthlessly paraded their prospects before me, and those more cunning who sought friendship with my sister to gain an introduction. The king had even hinted of a betrothal with his youngest daughter. An ideal partner, one of royal blood, said to be as lovely as she was sweet-tempered—one who might have bored me within the year. I had considered the proposal with detachment, weighing the privilege against my lack of enthusiasm. Yet I knew now with striking clarity that I would not join the king's family. I did not need the gifts his favor could bestow. The woman from yesterday had thrown my life's direction to the wind. What was it that lay between us? Impossible, that it was love after a day's acquaintance. More likely it was a passing fancy that would fade the more I learned of her, although my instincts recoiled at the thought. Whatever it was, I would seek my answers tonight.

In the courtyard, I strode over the arched bridge that led to the main pavilion. My eyes swept across it to ensure everything was in order. My sister often teased that I planned everything with meticulous precision. Before becoming a minister, I had served in the royal army, learning to swiftly ascertain the most advantageous terrain, the ideal conditions for attack or defense. While tonight was not a battle, the outcome was no less important. Not for the fleeting satisfaction of victory—though I relished that—but because I possessed a keen instinct for what was truly vital.

Rich sandalwood perfumed the air, wafting from the incense burners set along the pathway. I motioned to an attendant to remove them, preferring the crispness of the autumn breeze. Silk screens were artfully positioned, shielding us from the other patrons of the teahouse. Strings of lanterns swung from the branches above, aglow in shades of white and gold. All around the courtyard were flowers, vivid and fragrant. But the beauty that drew me back here each time lay in the mountains ringing the lake, reflecting the sun and moon in their majesty. I was neither poet nor artist, but this sight roused in me the desire to hold a brush, to try to capture the waves that melded with the skies, afire with an unearthly radiance.

If there was magic in our world, it must exist in this place.

Attendants arrived, bearing trays of food. They set the porcelain plates and bowls upon the marble table, each dish a famed delicacy of the place: roasted quail, chicken stewed with herbs, braised abalone, crisp crab claws, bamboo clams steamed with ginger, pastries filled with sweet lotus paste. A jug of wine was placed on the side, along with a pair of matched cups, and a black lacquered qin had been set on a side table.

As the attendants left, doubts plagued me. If she did not come, how would I find her? I did not even know her name—a ridiculous circumstance. How careless, to allow this slip. I had not been myself then, trying to understand the tumult of my emotions. An unbearable thought that she might be lost to me. I could not let that happen; I would find her again, no matter what stood in my way. Caution and reason no longer governed but something more profound, and far more chaotic. Glancing at the instrument, my fingers itched to play a song to settle my nerves—

Footsteps sounded; someone was approaching. To show haste would be indecorous, but I was too impatient to wait. I strode to the edge of the pavilion, my pulse racing like I was some inexperienced boy in the first flush of infatuation. There she stood, on the other end of the bridge, staring at me as I did at her.

Lotuses bloomed on the waters between us— late for the season—yet she cast them all into the shade. Her lips swept into a smile, set above the intriguing mark in her chin. A flaw, some might complain, but it lent her face a rare strength. Perhaps I was biased, inclined to turn all her faults into virtues—

and as I continued to gaze at her, a faint blush spread across her cheeks. She appeared my age, a little younger maybe, yet in her eyes swam a depth of knowing. I was familiar with the expression: of hope unconquered, of rising from the trials of suffering and loss. A tenderness swept through me. If she would allow me, I would help her heal and keep her safe. No one would hurt her again. The force of my emotions shook me once more. What could this be, if not love? But despite the unfathomable certainty that countered all sense, I would not be rash. I would not reveal these feelings too early, to make an unexpected move that might drive her away.

The clouds above were tinted bronze, sunlight deepening to amber. As she came toward me, her robe fluttered in the breeze. Flowers were embroidered upon the skirt in soft colors. I had never noticed such details in another's garments before, nor taken such pleasure in them. Drawing a slow breath, I went to meet her at the top of the bridge, careful to keep a respectful distance, yet as near as propriety would allow.

"Thank you for coming." I wanted to say more, to compliment her appearance, but flattery did not come easily to me, perhaps why they called me aloof.

"Of course, I came," she replied. "I keep my word."

"As do I," I said solemnly. "Are you cold? Would you like to sit inside the pavilion?"

"The wind does not trouble me." Her gaze shifted behind me. "It is as beautiful here as you said."

"Soon the moon will rise." We walked side by side across the bridge, the top of her head almost brushing my shoulder. "The view remains as lovely, though cast in a different light."

"The moon always gladdens me." Her face tilted up to mine. "I look forward to seeing it."

My spirits lifted, but I hid my pleasure as we entered the pavilion, gesturing to the dishes on the table. "I did not know what you liked—"

"—so, you decided to order everything," she interjected with a laugh.

I grinned, feeling more at ease. "I like to be prepared."

"I know. I mean . . . it's evident." Her face fell, a moment before she brightened again, an unexpected sheen glazing her eyes.

"Are you all right?" I asked gently. "You seem troubled."

"Only by the past. But it is the future now that matters."

I hesitated, forcing myself to overcome my instinctive reluctance to disagree with her. "The past is embedded in who we are, whether we choose to change or keep our course. Without our history, we are unmarked sheets of paper."

She met my gaze with a quiet calm. Few dared to look at me so, without shyness or calculation. "What about new beginnings?"

"Even those are bound to the past, for they cannot be new without the old. Whatever the past, it should not be ignored—but acknowledged, embraced, accepted. Only once we understand who we were, and what we are now, can we claim our future."

"You are right. Let us drink to that," she said fervently, lifting the jug of wine as she filled our cups. "To the days ahead."

I drained my cup, as did she. This wine was indeed one of the teahouse's best—mellow and sweet, while its fragrance was rich and full. Music rippled faintly through the air from the main hall of the teahouse. As her gaze fell upon the qin here, a strange wistfulness flashed across her face.

"Do you play?" I asked.

"A little, but I sorely lack practice."

"You are welcome to play with me. If you do not have an

instrument, I have several in my home." I fell silent, chiding my-self for moving too quickly beyond the bounds of courtesy. "My sister will be present," I offered to counter any doubts—though how she would laugh at my clumsiness tonight.

"Thank you, I would be glad to accept." She leaned across the table. "Will you tell me of your life here?"

To another, I would have been more guarded, yet such con-cerns fell away in her presence. "My parents were merchants, prosperous at first, but they ran into ill luck and lost their fortune. With their foresight, however, my sister and I were well-educated. I passed the king's examination, earning a place in his army, and later, at his court." I spoke lightly of my accomplishments, not wanting to dwell on them, eager to learn more about her.

"They called you a minister. What do you do?" she asked.

"I offer my advice on matters of state, guiding the king to the best of my abilities. Above all, I work to keep peace in the kingdom, unless it is threatened."

"Is peace important to you? What of power and ambition?" she pressed with sudden intensity.

I searched her face. "Do those things matter to you?"

"Should they not?"

I pondered her question, wanting to answer honestly. "They are important for what they can offer: freedom, security, respect. Yet everyone has a different dream, and part of life is deciphering what it is."

"Tell me about your dreams."

I marveled at how skilled she was at drawing the truth from me, even the parts I had never felt compelled to divulge before. "Will you share yours?" I countered.

When she nodded, I continued, "My dreams have changed since we met," I said bluntly. "Now, I want to spend each day as tonight."

A smile lit her face, yet she did not speak, her hands trembling as she clasped them on the table.

"Do my words frighten you?" I asked quietly.

"I don't frighten easily. I am . . . glad."

A sudden lightness filled me, as heady and sweet as the wine we had drunk. I refilled her cup, glad for the distraction. "Now it's your turn. Tell me about you—where you're from, your life, your dreams?"

"I want to be happy." It didn't escape my notice that she chose the question she wanted to answer. "For a long time, I didn't realize how precious happiness was, always pushing it away in place of greater or more pressing demands. I am learning to savor it, to cherish the feeling."

"And now?" I probed.

"I'm becoming selfish." She lifted the cup to her lips. "I do not want to relinquish it."

"Nor do I."

We fell silent, each of us seemingly turning over what the other had said.

"Do you have any regrets?" she asked.

"I've had to make hard choices, to put myself and my family above others. Fortune flows to those who claim it, unless you have the luck to be born to it." I spoke frankly, part of me fearing it might repulse her, but sensing she would value honesty above all.

"Do you wish you could change anything about your past?"

"No. Because it led me to you." As she flushed, I added, "These are no empty words; I mean what I say."

"You always do."

"Always?" I repeated curiously.

"I mean, you don't seem frivolous, saying one thing and meaning another." She spoke hastily, her throat convulsing.

I would not press her. "Tell me more about yourself."

"What else do you want to know?"

My gaze held hers. "Everything."

Her smile was almost tender. "It would take more time than we have tonight."

Her eyes flicked downward, her lips pressing together. Evasion, I recognized it well. She asked all of me but hid herself. She *had* been hurt, anger jolting me at the realization. Yet I would not press her. I would be patient and trust she would open herself to me in time.

"Then tell me the next day, or the day after that—for as many as you will grant me."

She slanted her head to one side. "We've only just met. How can you say such things?"

"I have never been afraid to speak my mind, to pursue what I want."

"Oh." A coolness drifted into her tone. "Have there been many 'pursuits'? Do you enjoy the chase?"

Did jealousy sharpen her tone? A fierce satisfaction gripped me at the thought. "It depends on the prey." My reply was designed to needle her, to read what I could in this unguarded moment.

Her eyes flashed as sharp as a blade. "I wish you luck, but I'm not interested in any hunt."

"I'll wager you're far too capable to be anyone's prey," I said with utter sincerity.

"What am I then?" A note of challenge rang out. This seemed almost a game, each of us unwilling to reveal too much of ourselves, yet daring the other to confess.

Though some secrets were better left undisturbed.

"I do not know yet," I said. "Except I would not take you for a butterfly or songbird. You are not one to be caged, nor to be another's ornament. Nor will I play games with you, for you are not a prize to be connived or won."

"Not an ornament. Not a prize." She repeated my words as she toyed with the rim of her cup. "If this is flattery, you need to improve upon it."

Her tone was arch as though she was now flirting with me. My heart leapt at the possibility. "Allow me the chance to practice, and I will not disappoint you."

Her eyes crinkled into crescents, as did her lips. How beautiful she looked in this moment, how utterly radiant.

"What I really think of you . . . I will not tell you tonight." Did I say this to intrigue her, to entice her to see me again? Or was I trying to understand my own feelings? More likely I was afraid of scaring her, for what I felt unnerved me, too.

"Do you speak this way to everyone?" she teased. "I thought you guarded when we first met. You did not even smile."

"I'm no flirt," I assured her. "Just as you are not *anyone*."

"You barely know me," she protested.

"Time is not the only measure of familiarity."

"Indeed," she agreed with feeling.

"Do you believe in the strings of fate?" What else might account for such strange emotions?

"That the Keeper of Mortal Fates is tying up little figures of us with red thread?" She laughed, shaking her head.

I frowned. "I have not heard of this Keeper of Mortal Fates."

"I speak in jest." She sounded somber now. "I do not believe in another fixing our destinies. I believe we make our own, and some of us might even defy that which is written in the stars."

"I would move the stars for you," I said quietly, as something shifted into place inside me. "I would defy them all."

She did not mock my declaration or question it, looking up at the sky, aglitter with light. "Let us leave the stars as they are, for tonight they are where they should be."

It was a solemn moment, as if something significant had passed between us—an unspoken promise, binding and eternal. Warmth flared in my chest, a sense of wholeness. Despite all I had achieved, I'd always felt something was lacking from my life. I had never believed in fate or destiny before, but what else might explain this bond, this feeling of rightness in being by her side—for now, for all our days to come. And though I did not know to which god I owed such generosity, I would strive to be worthy of it.

XINGYIN | 星银
HOME

The epilogue to the Celestial Kingdom duology.

———

SNOW LAY HEAVY UPON THE branches of the plum blossom tree. Clumps of ice clustered around the pink petals, a glittering frame to their beauty—all the more striking because of the barrenness surrounding it, the land stripped of its verdant glory.

Would I ever get used to the wintry chill? I wrapped my arms across my chest, wishing I had brought a cloak. While the cold did not harm me in this realm, it was not pleasant nonetheless. Yet I had grown to love the shifting of the seasons, like the world was shedding an old garment for the new. If the Celestial Kingdom was a garden in eternal spring, its beauty preserved like a bloom set in crystal, the Mortal Realm was change incarnate. Each season birthed new beauty and life, while burying the wear of the old—the cloying heat of summer giving way to the coolness of autumn. Leaves of green morphing to crimson gold, falling to the ground in crumpled heaps. Winter's frost creeping across the earth with relentless cruelty, plants withering, some never to sprout again. And then the renewal of the cycle once more, when the sun returned in force, the days stretching longer as the first daffodils sprang from the ground still silvered with ice.

With change came hope, riding upon the passage of time. Of new beginnings and second chances, rare and precious though they were.

Each year, another line was etched upon his beloved mortal face, another thread of white gleaming among his black strands . . . while I remained unchanged. I caught snatches of the attendants' gossip, their eager whispers drifting through the corridors. Some accused me of being a witch for beguiling their master, using potions and spells to keep time at bay. Others claimed more nefarious things: bargains with devils, that I was a malicious spirit in the guise of a mortal, leading their master to ruin. Such suspicious minds they possessed. And yet, I could not fault them entirely for they were both right and wrong. I was not a witch, nor was I mortal.

Had decades passed? It felt like a year. Time was an elusive thing for all its precision—happiness so fleeting, while sorrow dragged on like a path without end.

A breeze wound through the courtyard, catching my sleeves and skirt. The light was fading, the sun's rays dwindling with each passing moment. A blink, a breath, and the sky of plum and rose would lose its crisp luster, dusk softening to night. Stars flickered to life across the horizon, the moon casting its pale glow over this world. Closing my eyes, I inhaled the sweetness in the air, my mind tangling with the past as I instinctively searched for the fragrance of osmanthus. A memory slid into my mind, that of my mother standing upon the balcony of our home, her white robe gleaming as she leaned over the railing to gaze upon this place—the world of my parents. Yet no longer did regret gnaw at her heart, no longer did remorse press upon her. My parents were reunited, my family whole.

"Xingyin, are you not cold?" His voice was deep and resonant. While here he was known as Minister Zhao, to me he was forever Wenzhi. As he came toward me, his hand unclasped his woolen cloak. With gentle hands he draped it across my shoulders, the warm cloth sliding over me, its hem trailing across the frost riddled earth.

I should have returned it to him, but then I caught the faint scent of pine that clung to the cloak. Selfishly, I pulled it tighter around myself. My eyes met his, so dark yet overlaid with a sheen of brightness, almost silver in their hue. An unusual color in the Mortal Realm, though perhaps only an immortal's sight could discern this as no other had remarked on it. I drank in the sight of his handsome face, those thin lines stretched across his brow. His solemn expression that I had once thought forbidding and aloof—arrogant even, except when he looked at me as he did now. There was a new softness there, a curve to his mouth that pierced my heart. After all, it was not so long ago, I believed him lost to me.

"Thank you," I told him, as he sank down beside me on the wooden bench.

He nodded as he took my hand—his grip firm, his skin cool. "Why will you not marry me?" he asked directly, a question he had been asking more often of late. "We've lived together these past years, scandalizing the city." A smile formed on his lips, though his pupils glinted like iron. "They think you under my protection."

I shrugged aside these narrow thoughts, wedged between curiosity and spite. "They think worse of me than that." A woman of ill-repute. A temptress. An opportunist. Without even the title of "concubine" to clad my presence in a frail shroud of decency. Not that Wenzhi kept any here, for if he did—

My mind went blank, jealousy scraping my heart. But I cast

it aside for after all we had been through, I should be assured of his affection.

His face darkened. "I would never dishonor you so."

"If only you would." Heat flushed me as these words were inadvertently spoken aloud. Yet I held his gaze, refusing to flinch from my desires. If danger had taught me anything, it was not to shrink from life, to grasp opportunity and cherish each moment of happiness. Here, Wenzhi seemed to have far stricter morals. Though no less passionate, no less hungry for my touch than I was for his—there were boundaries he refused to cross, no matter the temptation. Perhaps in this mortal form, the rules of convention ingrained in his childhood bound him tighter. Or just as likely, he knew how much I wanted him, and was leaning on desire to bend me to his will. My teeth clenched at the thought. He was ever ruthless in his schemes, which was why he was so often victorious.

Light flared in his eyes as he brushed his knuckles down my cheek. "Then say yes," he whispered, leaning closer to me.

I sought escape in deflection. "Wouldn't you rather a younger wife who can bear your heirs?" My light tone concealed the tautness in my chest. In mortal years, he must think me far beyond the ideal age of a bride.

He drew back as though I had slapped him. "There is no one but you," he said fiercely. "There will never be anyone but you. You know I desire no other, that I want to be bound to you, alone. But only if you wish that, too."

Curt words, uttered in anger. Yet such warmth coursed through me upon hearing them. "What if I do not?" I asked archly. A new joy, this teasing between us, an ease to our interactions that had rarely existed when he was immortal. First, constrained by our positions in the Celestial Army, then shadowed by his betrayal.

"Then it does not matter what I want," he said.

As he looked away, I flushed at my flippant words. He knew nothing of our past; he did not feel the assurance I did, that our future lay beyond this mortal life span—that eternity was before us, the days stretching out like a dream without end. But time with him, whether transitory or not, was precious, and I would not waste it in needless conflict.

As though sensing the shift in my mood, he turned to me again. "Don't you want to prove the gossips wrong? To put their wagging tongues to rest, and shame them all to have to bow before you, when you are the mistress of this place?"

He knew my nature well to make such an argument. It would give me more than a little petty satisfaction, though I should not care what they thought when we would soon leave this realm. How easy it would've been to seize the happiness before us now. To call him "husband" and hear him speak the word "wife," whether tender with affection or rough with passion. To yield to the heat he stoked so effortlessly with a single touch, an assured slide of his hand along the curve of my back, as he pulled me to him with impatient urgency. His fingers buried in my hair or clasped tight around my waist. His mouth seeking mine with hunger, his callused palms scorching a path over my skin.

However, just as he had his principles, I had mine. And deep down, it felt wrong to bind him to me this way, without him knowing who he truly was . . . all we had been to each other. His betrayal and sacrifice, my hate and love—each a part that made us whole, entwined with what we were then, and all we had become. There were times I felt undeserving of this chance, that it was a fevered dream to have lived these decades with him, pretending our past did not exist. But part of him would not be enough. I wanted *all* of him, to know he still wanted me even after recalling everything that had transpired. If I was greedy, being with him had made me so.

"I don't care what they say." It came out more forcefully than intended. "The only opinions that matter are from those I care for." I repeated what he had told me once. Yet these words—though honest—were ill-chosen, for I had offered him the perfect weapon with which to strike.

His grip tightened over my hand as he drew me to him. "You are right. Not for them, but for us. You are free, as am I. Your heart is mine, as mine is yours." The resolve in his tone was implacable, without a trace of uncertainty. Perhaps this is what it would have been like had he not doubted my feelings from the start, his knowledge of my past stoking his jealousy—for his mind was one that trailed through the shadows, hearing all that remained unsaid, seeing what others wished they could conceal.

His head lowered to brush mine, his eyes darkening with intent. "Don't you want more than what we've had? Don't you want us to belong to each other in every way?" The low pitch of his voice thrummed through my body like a plucked cord.

I was caught in the moment, temptation coursing through me. Before I could reply, a shift in the air snared my attention. One I had almost forgotten, of power . . . magic . . . an immortal's aura drawing closer. A chill crept down my spine as I rose to my feet. Who had found us? One of Wenzhi's past enemies? One of mine? It did not matter. If they intended us harm, they would regret it. I reached for my magic, the tingling sensation almost unfamiliar, for it had been too long since I had need of it. Here, I abided by the Celestial Kingdom's rules; I would give no one cause to fault me. But in the next moment, my fears dispersed. That aura, golden bright and summer warm, was one I knew all too well.

Liwei. My first friend, my first love. And now, the Celestial Emperor whom the mortals revered, even if they did not know his true face or name. There was even an altar in the garden here, dedicated to the Emperor of Heaven, as he was known. The porcelain statue had a benevolent expression, a sweeping beard, a towering gold crown fixed upon his snowy head. I had burst out laughing when I'd seen it, to the chagrin and shock of the servants, no doubt solidifying their low opinion of me as ill-bred and impious. Perhaps they believed I would bring them misfortune through my irreverence. How I had wished that I could show the statue to Liwei, so we could laugh as we used to.

Yet Liwei was here now, my heart lifting at the thought. Light flared, illuminating the dark. I blinked, shielding my eyes, unaccustomed to the radiance after living among the mortals all these years. The wind whistled as a cloud swept down, Liwei standing upon it, clad in a silver brocade robe embroidered with twin dragons. His hair was pulled into a topknot, encased in a gold crown, not a hair out of place as he stepped to the ground. Whoever was attending to him now was more skilled than I had been, nostalgia enveloping me like mist.

Years had passed since we last met, when he'd told me of Wenzhi and healed the wounds in my heart. My chest twinged as I stared at his familiar face, both handsome and beloved, stirring precious memories. I was not made of stone, but I would not let my tenderness for the past confuse me again—my heart knew to whom it belonged. Yet beyond my gladness at seeing my friend, a spark of hope kindled at his presence, for I did not think this was an idle visit.

Too late did I sense Wenzhi's watchful stare upon me, his eyes narrowing as he rose and strode to Liwei.

"Noble Immortal, to what do we owe the honor of your presence?" His words were courteous, though his tone was cold as he remained standing, offering neither bow nor obeisance.

Even in his mortal form, he possessed the same self-assurance as before, caring little for another's position whether mortal or immortal, commoner or emperor. I hid my smile, for this was a trait we shared, believing respect should be earned, not granted.

"I am not here for you." Liwei nodded to me. "I am here for her."

"Why?" Wenzhi demanded. "If she has caused offense or broken a rule of heaven, let me settle the debt."

I glared at him. Did he think I would only cause trouble? Perhaps he had not forgotten *everything*, his instincts rising to the fore.

Liwei's mouth tilted into a tight smile. "You have given quite enough of yourself."

I shot him a warning look before reaching out to touch Wenzhi's arm. "There is no need for concern. Why don't you let us speak alone?"

"Are you sure?" Wenzhi asked. "I would not leave you in danger."

"He is a friend."

"*Friend?*" Liwei repeated, a trace of humor in his voice—and something else I was reluctant to dwell upon. "Surely we are more than that."

"You know him?" Wenzhi asked, yet it did not seem a question, his tone at once seeking and knowing.

"Oh, we know each other well," Liwei replied with an ease that irked me. "Far longer than you have known her."

"We are friends—" I repeated.

"—we are friends, *now*," Liwei interjected unhelpfully. Maybe this was small retribution on his part, for how Wenzhi had needled him in the past.

Anger clouded Wenzhi's gaze. I held his arm a little tighter before releasing it. "I will speak to him."

Wenzhi stared at Liwei, his head slanted back with evident disdain. "Hurt her, and you will suffer for it."

Part of me quailed to have him threaten the Celestial Emperor so, as Liwei's eyes flashed with rare anger. "Mind your manners, mortal. Do you know to whom you speak?" In these years we'd been apart, he had acquired a stern regality—an echo of his father's.

"You could be the Emperor of Heaven himself, but I care not what you think," Wenzhi replied icily.

Reckless words. I stared at Liwei, silently asking for tolerance. If a mortal had spoken to the previous Celestial Emperor in this manner, they would have promptly found themselves incinerated to a mound of ash. Liwei's fingers curled as he inclined his head. Once he might have drawn a sword on Wenzhi, but perhaps time had taught us all forbearance.

As Wenzhi strode away, toward the other side of the courtyard—Liwei's magic wound around us, weaving a shield of privacy. It was needed, for we had much to say that I could not share with Wenzhi yet.

"Xingyin, you look well," he said, in a softer voice than before.

"As do you." Warmth flooded my chest, to speak to him again.

He smiled. "Life here suits you."

"Being happy does." I spoke unthinkingly, as the corners of his mouth tightened. "I'm sorry, that was thoughtless of me."

"Never be sorry for it. You deserve to be happy; I want nothing less for you."

I blinked away the sudden prickling in my eyes. "I want you to be happy, too. If you ever need my help—"

His smile widened. "*You* are threat enough for my enemies, even as the number grows each day."

"A good ruler cannot avoid making them." I paused before asking, "Are you happy?"

He glanced up at the sky, his eyes fixed on the clouds. "Yes, I am. There are many types of happiness in the world. Some bring your entire self together, yet those also wield the power of breaking it apart. But there is happiness in smaller things too, that you can piece together to form a whole—no less strong or meaningful."

Silence cloaked us. No, I did not think he loved me anymore, not in that way—yet there would always be a touch of longing for our past that had shaped us both. Not regret, for my choice had been made a long time ago, as had his. How close we had been, I thought heavily. How I had loved him. And now, we were at once more and less than friends. There was a distance between us now riddled with faded hopes, a chasm of unfulfilled dreams. But other memories bridged the gap, warm and precious and much beloved—cords of friendship that could never be snapped.

"Aren't you curious, why I came?" he asked.

"Will you tell me?" My mind was already flying back to the day we had last spoken, recalling the promise he had made me then.

Liwei's hand slipped into his flowing sleeve, drawing something out. A jade bottle, ornamented with gold filigree. A sweetness drifted through the air, the familiar fragrance of peaches. This was the same elixir of immortality that had separated my parents, before finally reuniting them. The only thing in the world I desired now, the key to Wenzhi's restoration—to our future.

"The elixir is ready. It is yours."

He did not toy with me, nor did he make any demands, offering it with the graciousness I had loved in him . . . that I would always cherish him for. My mouth went dry, a torrent of emotion swelling in my chest—the heady lightness of hope, along with a raw ache from wanting.

"Liwei, thank you. I am grateful." I stumbled over my words, chaotic and graceless. "What can—"

He tucked the bottle into my palm, folding my stiff fingers across it. "There are no debts between us. Find your happiness."

"You must find yours, and not just in your duty," I told him fervently. "Your parents' union need not be yours. Any immortal would leap at the chance to wed you." The old hurt throbbed still, like the shadow of a wound that had not quite healed. Liwei was a part of me, he always would be—and I was grateful for it, for him . . . for us.

"Any immortal, except for one." His gaze did not leave mine as he smiled, and despite the echo of wistfulness there was no longer any hurt.

"Any *wise* immortal," I clarified, returning his smile.

He shook his head. "There is still much to do before I turn my mind to such matters. But rest assured that General Jianyun will not let me forget my duty to ensure the line of succession. He has already drawn up a list of prospects."

"Do not think of it as a duty," I said quietly. "You deserve far better. While love sometimes strikes unaware, it can also be cultivated. Choose with your heart, not just your mind."

"And if I do not?" he asked, his eyes crinkling.

"Then I will pay General Jianyun a visit."

Liwei laughed, a welcome sound, breaking the last of the tension between us. His gaze shifted to a point behind me. "Your beloved is showing remarkable patience by allowing us to speak so intimately—not stalking over here and challenging me as he once did."

"You had your hand in instigating those confrontations," I reminded him tartly.

"He deserved it."

"Oh, he did then," I agreed wholeheartedly. "But not anymore. Moreover, you are the virtuous and benevolent Celestial Emperor, and your conduct must match your lofty position." I gestured toward the statue in the garden.

As Liwei's gaze followed mine, his eyes bulged. "I must have a word with the Keeper of Mortal Fates. This is . . . this is . . ."

"A remarkable likeness? I thought it did you justice," I observed innocently.

"Did you *buy* that statue to annoy me?" Liwei demanded.

I lowered myself into a mocking bow. "I did not, Your Celestial Majesty. Though I will now ask for it to be elevated to a pedestal and send for more such likenesses to be crafted in your honor."

"I will strike them all down," he threatened, even as his mouth twitched.

"You must not frighten the mortals," I warned him. "Don't forget your own rules."

"One of them being that you should not be here," he reminded me.

"I am grateful for Your Celestial Majesty's patience." My hand tightened around the elixir, a lump rising in my throat. "And I am grateful that we can now return."

A brief silence ensued. "I must go, but I will see you in the skies above. If the Demon—if *he* does anything to hurt you, I will send him back to the Mortal Realm as an insect," he warned, before adding, "Though you never needed me to fight your battles."

He faced Wenzhi then, inclining his head gravely in farewell. Without another word, Liwei stepped upon the cloud that hovered by his feet, soaring into the heavens.

Wenzhi stalked toward me, each step brisk with impatience. In these years, he had always respected my wishes, even when they conflicted with his—though he'd undoubtedly tried to convince me of his way.

"Who was he?" he wanted to know.

"Did his presence bother you?" I asked curiously. He would not remember Liwei, nor was he inclined to jealousy.

A line creased his brow, finer ones forming at the corners of his eyes like he was trying to recall something. "It might be the way he was looking at you, or how you were looking at him. Whatever it was, I did not like him. Nor did he like me."

"There is no reason to be concerned," I assured him. "He has done us a great favor. One we can never repay."

"You are speaking in riddles today, Xingyin." His gaze pinned mine though he did not demand an explanation. Perhaps he was used to my half-formed thoughts, the sentences I cut short abruptly for there were times I let things slip that I should not have. While I was no stranger to deception, I was careless with those I allowed into my heart.

Tonight, I would cast aside the veil of secrecy I had always worn here. Tonight, I would answer all his questions, and learn the answer I had been anticipating and dreading in equal measure: Did Wenzhi still love me in his true form? A chill darted over me as I raised my head to the sky. Stars glimmered, strewn across the silken night. The moon was luminous, the light of a thousand lanterns shining down on us. Perhaps my parents had lit them together, and I drew both solace and strength from the thought.

"These past years, you asked me many questions—some of which I did not answer: Why I never fell ill? Why I called you 'Wenzhi' on occasion? Where I was from? Why could we not wed?" I began haltingly. "You did not pry, even as you knew I was hiding something. And you were right, except it was not just *my* past I was concealing."

He leaned closer to me. "Will you tell me now?"

"Do you trust me?" I asked.

"Yes," he replied. "For I have never known you to lie."

My nose wrinkled involuntarily, memories flashing through me of the time I had drugged him, the lies I had spoken then and after—even as I'd tried to deceive myself as to the workings of my own heart.

"Though you might change the subject, or refuse to answer a question, or bend the truth on occasion," he added lightly, before his expression turned solemn. "There is no one I trust more than you."

I prayed his conviction would hold. "You and I are not of this realm. We belong to the skies, where *he* came from."

Wenzhi's eyes narrowed, his mind working as he weighed my words, preposterous though they might sound to any mortal. Perhaps if he had not seen Liwei descend upon the cloud, he might be more inclined to disbelief. "I do not think you are jesting with me," he said slowly. "That would mean you are speaking the truth, or what you believe to be true."

"It *is* the truth. Look at me." I raised my hand, cradling his beloved face. "Over these decades, while time has left its marks on you, have you noticed any changes in me? I never suffer any ailment, any wound nor illness, for nothing harms me here."

"What are you?" His voice was steady, his gaze intense.

"Do you believe me a monster? A witch, as so many think?" I spoke brightly to conceal my trepidation. Part of me wanted to keep things as they were; we were happy now, cocooned in ignorance, severed from past entanglements and strife. What might happen if these were unearthed again? What if he did not love me after regaining his memories? What if he blamed me for pushing him aside until it was too late? Yet greater than this cowardly urge was the desire to move onward, to claim the life we should have lived.

"My sister thinks you are a sorceress. Is she right?"

"Would it matter?" I countered.

He shook his head without hesitation. "I don't see you with my eyes. I feel you here." His hand pressed his chest. "If you are a monster, let me be one, too. Though if you are a witch, it would explain the spell you've cast on me since the day we met," he said with a grin.

"I've been called worse," I admitted. *And so have you.* Liar. Traitor. Demon. By every Celestial who knew his name. By myself when I'd cursed him in those weeks and months when my pain was still raw, the wounds of his betrayal raked fresh across my heart.

Back then, I had not thought they would ever heal, that we would ever come to this, that we would walk our path together once more. I had not made the decision lightly to spend these years with him, yet my fears had been too great. What if he should bind himself to another in this mortal life? One who would love him better than I had, whom he might start a family with. One who would have greater claim over his affection, who would replace me in his heart once he regained his immortality. Could I bear losing him again? And so, selfish creature that I was, I had claimed him here—to be with him for as long as I could, to seize the happiness before me, transitory and fleeting though it might be. I banished the remaining flickers of doubt; I would not regret the past, nor would I question the future. I would face it as I had everything before, even as my heart raced, my palms turning cold.

I extended my hand, offering him the jade bottle. "This is the Elixir of Immortality. Drink it and you will remember everything. You will become who you were, restored to your true immortal form."

He did not move, his gaze fixed upon me. "Will we remain as we are?"

"I don't know," I replied honestly. "Though I wish it more than anything."

His eyes dropped to the bottle in my grasp. "I do not want it if it means losing you."

"You will not lose me." A fullness rose in my throat that he would disdain immortality for our love. I pressed the bottle into his hand. "If you want, we will have everything we had here, and more. Eternity lies before us. Family. Home."

He nodded then, plucking the gold stopper from the bottle. The fragrance that spilled forth was so rich, it was almost overwhelming. As he raised the bottle to his lips and tipped it back, I closed my eyes. His breathing quickened, though there was no gasp nor sigh of discomfort. The elixir was true. With Liwei, there would be no hidden strings, no price to be paid, no demand of service to the Celestial Kingdom. He was not his father.

The air rippled with the force of Wenzhi's aura, powerful and steady. A coolness glided over my skin like a breath of autumn, thick with the scent of rain, leaves . . . and change. As my eyes flew open, he spoke my name.

"Xingyin."

His voice was different from what it had been here—deeper, suffused with knowing. A trace of disbelief . . . and infinite relief.

My gaze fell into his. Bright like molten silver, that of rainfall on a wintry evening. Like frost and ice and starlight, crushed into a wealth of glittering shards. It was *him*, no longer just the mortal I had spent these years with, but the immortal I had trusted then hated, cursed and wept over . . . then fallen in love with all over again. He had been too ambitious and ruthless before, while I had been stubborn and unforgiving. We had been buried in deceit and lies then, smothering any seed of truth in our relationship. Change was not something an immortal was accustomed to, yet the hurt we'd wrought on each other had remade us from within. We had been tested, broken, and forged anew into something stronger.

And we belonged together.

Recognition dawned in his face. Did he finally see *all* of me, our past and present as one? His hands reached for mine, his grip cool and fierce. How I had ached for his remembered strength, and while he had embraced me countless times over these years, his touch was now hesitant—like this was a dream he was afraid to wake from.

"I remember," he said in wonder. A shadow crossed his face before it was dispelled by his smile. "If this is death, I am content."

"You are alive. We are alive." How I wanted to laugh and cry from the sheer opulence of the emotions that crashed over me. This weightlessness in my chest, this tingling warmth that grazed my skin, smoothing the creases and folds within—until

I was shivering though I was not cold, trembling though I was not afraid.

"All this time, you stayed with me in this realm. We were together. Why?" His tone was grave as he searched my face.

"There was nowhere else I wanted to be." I would hide nothing. "When I believed you dead, it was then I knew."

"What did you know?" How relentlessly he pried away each truth of my heart.

"That I love you," I told him without flinching. "Perhaps even before, though I did not want to admit it."

His eyes blazed till they seemed glazed by moonlight. "Do you forgive me?"

"Yes. A long time ago." Somehow, I managed to speak through the emotions that gripped every part of me.

He stilled . . . and then he clasped me to him—and I was holding him, too, so close, not a wisp of light could slide between us.

Nothing would come between us again.

Yet I would not be so foolish to think that; nothing was perfect in love nor life. These moments were to be cherished, branded into our memories, for they gave us the strength to face the trials that might come after. As long as we were together, we could endure anything that came our way.

My vision was blurred from tears. "Let us go home."

"Home," he repeated, resting his chin on my head. "And where would that be?" His words arched into a question, seeking out my desires.

I turned my face up to his, speaking each word gravely. "Wherever you are, whether you are Celestial or Demon, mortal or immortal."

A slow smile spread across his face as his arms tightened around me, the coolness of his skin a balm to the warmth of mine. "I did not think this day would ever come, though I had hoped for it with every breath, since the day you left," he whispered into my ear, his breath kindling a fire in my veins.

I raised my hand to trace his face, unlined once more, silken to my touch. His hair was now as black as mine, gone were those strands of white though I had grown to love them, too, as I did all the parts of him—even those deemed less than perfect. My hand shook from the freedom of touching him this way, the exquisite joy of knowing the last of the walls had come down between us.

As he bent his head to mine, his hands clasping my waist, mine went to his shoulders, winding around his neck. His lips sought mine with a fierce hunger, heat rushing through my body as I arched myself to fit him tighter. His heart pounded hard and fast against my chest—it was like we were kissing for the first time . . . perhaps, in a way we were, discovering each other anew. I closed my eyes to savor the feel of his body, the intimate press of his lips, his cool touch inflaming my desires as his hands clasped me to him, one curving around the back of my neck in a possessive hold that stole my breath and weakened my limbs. If he had not held me, I would have fallen. My senses were alive, afire with the light of the heavens. Darkness would never claim me again.

I did not know how long we remained this way, careless in our union, impatient and eager. At last, we broke apart, recalling where we were, that any of our attendants might have come across us.

"We should return to our realm—if the mortals see me this way, it will raise too many questions. But first, there is something I must do." He strode to the pavilion where a lacquered tray of writing materials was laid out. Taking a sheet of paper and a brush, he dipped it into the ink and wrote several lines of characters with his usual bold and sweeping strokes. When he was done, he pressed his personal seal upon the paper, folded it, and left it on the table.

"I am leaving all my possessions to my sister," he explained. "I will miss her, and am glad to have known a true sibling bond. I told her I'm retiring to a quiet life, one without need of material possessions."

"A quiet life?" I repeated in disbelief, recalling the monsters we had slain, the battles we had fought. The turmoil and chaos left in our wake.

His eyes flicked toward me, glinting with amusement. "An improbability with you, yet I would have it no other way."

As he raised his hand, the wind churned, a violet-gray cloud sweeping down by our feet. How I had missed the familiar rush of his power, the comfort of it closing around me. His fingers twined between mine, as we stepped upon the cloud. As the wind surged, it soared into the skies. There was no need for words; we had spoken them all, our hearts unfettered from the burdens of the past.

And as night cloaked the sky, never had it seemed so bright, incandescent with possibilities as infinite as the stars.

ACKNOWLEDGMENTS

This book would not exist without my editors. Thank you so much, David Pomerico, for your vision for this collection and your trust in my stories; it's an honor to work with you and your team. To Lara Baez, Rachel Weinick, and Mireya Chiriboga—you're all wonderful and I appreciate your help. Much gratitude also to Jeanne Reina, Abigail Marks, Jennifer Chung, Sarajane Herman, and Liate Stehlik.

My deepest thanks to the amazing Harper Voyager UK team: Natasha Bardon, Kate Fogg, Fleur Clarke, Kimberley Atkins, Elizabeth Vaziri, Susanna Peden, Maddy Marshall, Ellie Game, Chloe Gough, Leah Woods, and Robyn Watts. And, of course, to Vicky Leech Mateos. I'm grateful to everyone at HarperCollins in the US and UK, Canada, Australia, and internationally who worked on the books and helped bring them to the shelves. And to the publishers who translated the duology and the international distributors of the books, for helping them reach readers around the world.

To my agent, Naomi, for being an invaluable guide and partner throughout my author journey—for your steadiness, support, and advice.

It was very moving to see the stories brought to life by the incredible Kelly Chong, from the stunning US cover, to the exquisite illustrations in the book—I love them so much. Thank you, Jason Chuang, for the wonderful illustration of the beautiful UK cover, symbolic in many ways, that matches the others so well. Much gratitude also to Virginia Allyn for the breathtaking map, and to Natalie Naudus and Ewan Chung for the wonderful narration, bringing the characters to life.

I'm a great fan of FairyLoot and adore their stunning editions of *Daughter of the Moon Goddess* and *Heart of the Sun Warrior*, and now, *Tales of the Celestial Kingdom*. Thank you so much, Anissa and the FairyLoot team—it's an absolute dream to work with you and Grace Zhu, who illustrated the beautiful hardback foil and endpapers.

Words can't express how much I appreciate my husband's unwavering support, for always stepping in to help with the children, for reading all I write. And to my family and friends who have stood by me through the ups and downs—you keep me grounded and I am so glad you're in my life.

To all the booksellers and librarians, I am so grateful for your support and many kindnesses, for giving me a glimpse of the book in the stores and libraries when I can't be there. Thank you for everything you do for authors!

And last but definitely not least, my deepest gratitude to all the readers, creators, and artists who shared about the books on BookTok, Bookstagram, YouTube, and other platforms, who've recommended the stories, and created reels, videos, and art— you have all helped keep the books alive, making it possible for me to write more. So many of you have touched me with your posts and stories, and even brought me to tears with your heartfelt messages. To my readers, I am forever grateful—you inspire me to write.

ABOUT THE AUTHOR

Sue Lynn Tan is the author of the Celestial Kingdom duology. Her books have been translated into sixteen languages, are *USA Today* and *Sunday Times* bestsellers, and have been nominated for several awards. Born in Malaysia, Sue Lynn studied in London and France, before moving to Hong Kong. When not writing or reading, she enjoys exploring the hills, lakes, and temples around her home.

Find her on Instagram @suelynntan, or on her website www.suelynntan.com.

ABOUT THE ILLUSTRATOR

Hailing from a quaint Malaysian town, **Kelly Chong** is an illustrator with a graphic design degree from Coventry University. Her passion lies in seamlessly merging digital and traditional mediums, drawing inspiration from both Eastern and Western artistic traditions. She holds deep admiration for luminaries such as Harry Clarke, Kay Nielsen, and Edmund Dulac.